The Hurricane Party

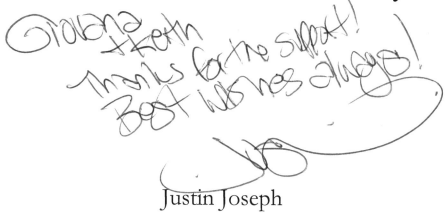

Justin Joseph

The following is a work of fiction. Names, characters, places, and incidents either are products of the author's imagination or are used fictiously. Any resemblance to actual events or locales or persons, living or dead, is entirely coincidental.

The Hurricane Party
The Last Meal of George Mills
Copyright © 2017 Justin Joseph
All rights reserved.
ISBN: 1975982355
ISBN-13: 978-1975982355

DEDICATION

Dedicated to my father, Ralph Vilonna.
Thanks for the support and love.
You are one of the greats.

ACKNOWLEDGMENTS

Special thanks to my loving wife, Celeste, for all of her love and support.

Thanks to Travis J Maynard and Tristan Gautreau for their input with the cover, as well as their priceless feedback regarding the following stories.

The author assumes all responsibilities for any and all mistakes.

Finally, thank YOU for reading and please enjoy.

"I'm on my own against the world…
And I've never felt so fucking cold."
-Carpathian

JUSTIN JOSEPH

THE HURRICANE PARTY

JUSTIN JOSEPH

CHAPTER 1
THE GANG'S ALL HERE

"It's the end of the world!" Danny screamed at the top of his lungs. He then proceeded to shake and then crack open a can of beer. Beer erupted out of the can and into the air splashing on everything and everyone in front of him. Everyone meaning, Jake, his wife Amy, their little boy Lance, and Danny's girlfriend Molly. Some beer splashed down on Danny and Molly's dog, Chopper. He didn't seem to mind, he was just happy to be there. A drop touched the couple's cat, Pepper, on her front right paw. She minded very much, so, she exited the room in an extreme rush.

"Danny!" Molly screamed. "Stop it! You're making a mess!"

" ess," Lance repeated after Molly as he proceeded to splash his milk everywhere.

"Yes, *mess*," Amy said acknowledging her son's effort to learn the English Language. "But we don't do that, Lancey dear. OK?"

"K," Lance said and looked elsewhere.

Jake smiled at the chaos that was around him and took a chug of his own beer.

"What?" Danny said to Molly with a sly little smile. "I'm just having fun." He held up his beer and looked around the table. "To the end of the world, let's make this the best hurricane party ever!"

"Cheers to that," Jake said.

"Cheers," Molly whispered as she began to clean up Danny's mess.

" 'eers," Lance spoke up.

"Yes, *cheers*, honey," Amy said to her son. "Very good! *'eers*!"

The crew was huddled up around Danny and Molly's kitchen table. They all took a sip of their beers. Jake smacked his lips. The beer was exactly what he needed. It had been a rough last few days. Hurricane preparations always took their toll on you prior to any storm. Jake was 35 years old. Sandy blonde hair, clean shaven with an athletic yet dad bod build. He was just less than 6 feet tall. He used to be very active, but married life, his job, and now kid took away his free time for such activities such as volley ball, skateboarding, and even jogging. His wife, Amy, was shorter than him, had a problem with losing the baby weight and had kind of given up on slimming down. To be fair, she had tried everything. From breast feeding to diets to exercise and even fasting. Nothing worked. So she was just going with the flow. Now, she was not obese, she just had an extra few pounds on her. The thing was, despite what Amy thought, it looked good on her. She could pull it off. Jake did not care about the weight, because that did not matter to him at all. All he cared about was his wife's happiness. Amy had a pretty face. She was one of those girls that could rock any hair style and any hair color. Long and dark? Amy looked beautiful. Short and blonde? Amy looked stellar. What really got Jake though was Amy's sense of humor. It was dry and at times dark, which to Jake was epic. 27 months ago, Lance was born and the couple's life was turned upside down with overwhelming love and affection. Lance was a gift from the Heavens. Jake and Amy's relationship was going smooth before they found out that they were going to be parents. Lance just made it that more magical. Sure, there were tough times, there always are with an infant, and Lance was a hyper little dude. But it added spice and adventure to the life of Jake and Amy. They wouldn't have it another way. Lance had Amy's cute little face and Jake's blonde hair. He was a smart kid as well as good looking. Unlike many children his age, Lance was able to occupy himself with a book or crayons and a sketch pad. Jake and Amy were blessed. They knew this and were grateful.

"Thank you for having us over, guys," Amy said.

"Of course!" Molly said and placed her hand on Amy's shoulder. "It wouldn't be a party without you three!"

"Yeah," Danny agreed. "Thanks for making it out." He looked over at Lance who was now using his red crayon as if it was going to disappear. Danny smiled. "Whatcha drawing, Lance?"

"Almo," Lance replied without bringing neither his eyes nor his crayon up from the paper.

"Almo?" Danny repeated looking at Jake for help translating.

"*Elmo*," Jake translated. "He is drawing Elmo."

Danny cocked his head to look at the drawing better. At first it seemed like the drawing was just a mess of red jagged lines. After a moment of letting it sink in that it was supposed to be Elmo, Danny could understand the child's thought process.

"Oh, wow," Danny mused. "Look at that. It is Elmo. Kid certainly has the red part down pat." Danny smiled at Jake.

"Yup. The kid loves Elmo," Jake said, smiling back to his friend.

Jake met Danny when they played in the same band, a punk band called Memory Debt, together in their youth. Jake played guitar, Danny played the bass and sang. Their one time friend Chaz played the drums but since then Chaz, who was the mutual friend that introduced the two, found the Lord and moved to Missouri to be a reverend. Though Jake and Danny had been through a lot together, the two friends were in fact nothing alike- Jake was into being active, while Danny was more into being a couch potato. Jake liked to listen to other genres of music, while Danny listened strictly to punk rock Jake liked to read novels, Danny read comic books. They had their differences but yet they hit it off just fine. They both had integrity and respect for one another. Plus, compassion for each other. Danny was shorter and stockier than Jake. He had pitch black hair and a poor attempt at a beard. Danny was a complete nerd. A geek with a huge comic book, DVD and toy collection. Everything he owned was either limited edition or rare, or at least that is what it said on the box. But this was what Danny lived for. Jake lived for his family, Danny lived for his collectables. To each their own. Jake loved Danny for who he was- an amazing friend with a huge heart. Jake was happy to see his friend happy with such an amazing girl whom was Molly.

In Jake and Amy's eyes Molly was a saint (for putting up with Danny's antics and collections and odd humor, the girl was certain to obtain sainthood). Danny and Molly had been together for just about as long as Jake and Amy had been and still no talk of marriage, kids or even buying their own home. To some women, this would all be a big problem, a deal breaker. However, Molly did not care about any of that, she loved Danny for Danny and that was that. Danny got lucky with her because Molly was the absolute definition of the girl next door. She was an all American girl. In high school, while Danny lit things on fire and threw vegetables at cars passing by, Molly was on the cheer squad and had straight A's. Molly had a warm smile that made everyone that met her feel like they had been friends forever. To put it plain- Molly was breathtakingly beautiful, inside and out.

Danny sipped his beer and looked at Jake. "Thanks again for helping me with the shutters, man."

"No biggie," Jake said.

Though it was a biggie. It was a gigantic biggie. In helping Danny with his shutters, Jake and Amy's home now sat without any shutters at all. And dear wife Amy was not happy at all with dear husband Jake. Jake, however, could care the less. The week prior to the arrival of Hurricane Elliott, Amy sat at home playing with Lance and watching her shows, meanwhile, Jake was out working his normal 9-5 crap job *and* gathering up all the supplies that they needed for the big natural event. Jake was in customer service for his day job and had to deal with the most mind numbing idiotic questions all day long. On top of the customer stupidity he had to deal with, he now had to go and fight the public for supplies; such as water, canned food, batteries, gas, and all of the other hurricane survival essentials. He was about to buy plywood for their house but Jake went to Danny's after work instead for a breather. When he got there, Molly was in hysterics and Danny was struggling putting up the shutters himself. Danny asked Jake for help with shuttering up his house. Jake thinking he was doing the right thing, said yes. The Hurricane was on its way and Danny's scumbag landlord refused to put up shutters. Danny told him to go fuck himself and got the plywood himself. "It's coming off our check, Don." Danny told his landlord. When Jake arrived, Danny was fuming and in the midst of trying to get the plywood up. Danny was not the most tool savvy guy so Jake jumped right in, wearing his work clothes and all (he removed his tie though. Fuck ties.)

"Yeah," Amy chimed in. "Thanks. Now our house has no shutters up. Awesome." Amy was very generous with her sarcasm and made no attempt at hiding her frustration that she had with Jake.

"We have insurance," Jake said. "I called the company two days ago to make sure everything was in order. It is. We will be fine. Besides, our place was built after the big one a few years back, so everything is to code. The place is basically hurricane proof." Jake took a sip of his beer and smiled smugly. "Ain't no thang, babe. Elliot is just a little bitch." Jake kissed his wife and wished that statement to be true.

Only a mere few hours ago, hurricane Elliot ripped through the Caribbean like a Mack truck running over a carton of eggs. There was not much news about the effect of the hurricane but rumor had it the damage was catastrophic and the death toll was high. This was no sleeper hurricane. It was headed straight up the middle of Florida as a category 5. According to the National Weather Bureau- *a category 5 hurricane is a major weather event with winds 157 mph or higher as well as severe rainfall. Hurricanes that reach category 3 and higher are considered major and can cause significant damage to properties as well as inflecting harm to life that can be potentially fatal.* The last report the gang had heard reported that Hurricane Elliot's winds averaged 163 mph and it was headed straight for them and their cozy little town of Lake Falls, Florida.

"Where the hell is Melissa and Captain Useless?" Jake asked.

"Jake!" Amy scolded her husband while giving him a look to tone it down.

"What?" he glanced at her and took a sip of his beer. "You know that kid is completely useless. Everyone does. Right, Danny?"

"Yup," Danny said and took a sip of his beer. "It has come straight out of his own mouth. Last time we all hung out he told me that he has no ambition to do anything with his life, at all. He just loves being lazy. I am honestly shocked that he has not gone out and bought velcro shoes for himself. Or even adult diapers."

"Yuck," said Molly. "That is just gross, Danny."

"Gross but true," Danny said.

"Yeah, I wouldn't put any of that past him," Jake said. "He is a real piece of work. I don't know where my cousin finds these guys. Like, they aren't even douchebags, they are somehow *worse*. They are like the *packaging* for a douchebag that you throw away. Just useless trash. Pure garbage."

"Yeah, but Melissa loves him," Amy said and then stopped herself. "Umm, I think she loves him?"

"I don't know how she can," Jake said. "The kid brings nothing to the table. He is a slacker. His goal is to never leave the house. It is amazing he goes to work at all."

"Where does he work again? I forget," Molly said.

"Panera Bread," Jake said. "Bus boy. Part time. Meanwhile my cousin busts her ass in the bank trying to make ends meet."

"Yeah, but they are young still," Molly said.

"No. My *cousin* is young," Jake said. "She is 24. *He* is 33."

"Oh, wow. He is almost our age," Molly said. She had a hint of sympathy in her voice.

"Yeah, '*Oh, wow*' is right," Jake said. He shook his head and frowned. "Whatever. She is happy though. That is all that matters, right?"

"That is right," Amy said. "That *is* all that matters. So mind your business, Jake. Just let her be happy. If he fucks up and hurts her-" Danny interrupted Amy.

"We beat his fucking ass," Danny said and drank his beer.

"Yup," Jake said as he pointed his beer in Danny's direction with a wink.

Amy sighed and rolled her eyes. "Yeah, that," she said.

Molly shook her head and smiled. "Boys will be boys."

"Yeah, I guess we will," Jake began. "That doesn't mean-" Jake was interrupted by the door bell ringing.

"Oh, snap," Danny said. "They are here." He looked at Jake with a smile. "Shush up and drink your beer, sweet heart."

"Yes, dear," Jake said. He drank his beer and flipped Danny the bird.

"I'll get the door," Molly said. She put down her beer and walked to the front door. It was quiet in the home but once Molly opened the door the group could hear the wind blowing outside. The storm was getting worse. Elliot was right on time.

"Is there even any parking out there?" Danny asked. "This place is always jammed packed." It was true. Danny and Molly's apartment complex was always chock full of cars and guests. Sometimes guests would park up over the curb on the grass or even double park in some cases. There was never enough parking in the complex Danny and Molly lived in.

"I got a spot just a few spaces down from yours," Jake said. "No biggie."

"Well good," Danny said. "I just hate to hear that you walked a bit to get here. Like last time. That sucked."

"Sure did," Jake said. The last time that they were over it *did* suck. Jake and Amy had to park a few *blocks* over from Danny and

Molly's home. Normally this wouldn't be a big deal but now Jake and Amy had to lug around Lance and all of his toys and activities- to put it simply, it was a chore. When they left, Danny helped Jake and Amy with all their stuff. It convinced him into never wanting to have children of his own for it was "just too much damn work."

Melissa and her boyfriend, "Captain Useless" himself, Matt entered the room. Matt nodded and shook everyone's hands, even the girls (a practice that was frowned upon within the group. They had all hung out before; it was acceptable to hug one another now).

Matt was a stocky guy. Clean shaven with curly brown hair. He looked flushed and this told Jake and Danny that Matt was not as lucky with finding a parking spot as Jake was- Captain Useless had to walk.

Seeing Matt next to Melissa made zero sense as to why they were a couple. Looks wise, Melissa was one hundred times out of his league. Melissa was, like Jake said, 24 years old, but she looked no older than 15. She was a gorgeous girl. Smooth skin and big beautiful eyes. Melissa was a petite little woman which made her even that more special to look at. Every feature she possessed was tiny and soft. Even her *voice* was tiny and soft. "Hey guys," Melissa said. "I made a cake for the party." She smiled and placed a cake down on the middle of the table. It was a rectangular layer cake with vanilla frosting. On the cake was a crudely drawn middle finger and written in elegant hot pink frosting were the words *FUCK ELLIOTT*.

"Ha! No way!" Danny said. "I love it. Though I think you misspelled *Elliot*. I think in this case it is one "T", not two. But regardless. Yeah, fuck Elliot indeed. With one T or two T's, fuck them both."

"Fuck yeah," Jake said. He smiled, tipped his beer in Danny's direction and then drank it down. Jake was getting a nice buzz on.

"We've got some pizza in the kitchen, if anyone wants," Molly said. "Help yourselves. Beer is in the fridge."

"Get it while it is cold!" Danny said. Everyone looked at him like he was nuts. "The beer! Not the pizza! Sheesh." Everyone laughed and smiled at each other except for Matt, Captain Useless.

"I'll take some pizza," Matt said and made his way to the kitchen by himself. Jake shot Danny a look, Danny smiled and Amy nudged Jake in the ribs giving him dirty eyeballs insinuating "Don't you start.

Don't you fucking dare." Jake looked at her and flashed his "Don't worry, babe, I know better" smile that he was ever so famous for.

"You know, I guess I could eat, too," Danny said.

"Me too," Molly said. "Better eat now while the power is still on. Eating in the dark sucks. Even if by romantic candle light." Molly motioned her hand towards the army of candles on the kitchen table. Amy smiled at her.

"Sounds like a plan. I think I will grab a slice or two as well," Jake said getting up out of his chair. He took a sip of his beer and placed the bottle down on the table. "You want a slice, babe?"

"Sure," Amy said. "Thanks. Oh! And another brewski, please."

"Same as last time?"

"Yup, same."

"Everyone! Shut up! Shut up! Shush!" Danny yelled out. Everyone looked at each other and froze. It was silent in the house, and all the group could hear was the wind howling and rain falling outside. Danny smiled a big shit eating grin at everyone. "You hear that?" Danny said. "It's Elliott. He's *here*."

CHAPTER 2
A HARD RAIN IS GOING TO FALL

As the group ate their pizza and made small talk, the storm outside became more aggressive. Dead palm fronds fell to the wet earth making a splashing and heavy leafy sound as they hit the concrete. The fronds would then move by force of the wind down the sidewalks and roads, twisting and turning over themselves. Twigs and leaves joined the fronds as they slid and tumbled over and through puddles and crab grass. The rain fell hard and without mercy. The wind pushed the rain in what seemed like every direction. For a while, the wind would blow East, and the rain would follow, then, South. Then North. Then it would turn on a dime back East, then back to spray towards the West. There was no method or reason to the wind, only the method of destruction. Wooden fences shook in their place like church goers receiving the Holy Spirit from their minister. Unattended garbage pails rolled down the roads and alleyways, bumping and smashing whatever was in their way. The litter of yesterday flew and swooped in the air. Plastic wrappers, discarded coffee cups, and empty potato chip bags all joined the palm fronds, twigs and leaves down the road in a merry parade of debris. Inside the house, all of this went unnoticed thanks to the plywood shutters. Well, mostly all of it.

"Sheesh," Jake said. "Hear that wind?"

"Yup," Danny said. "I guess that is what 150 mph winds sound like, huh?"

"Actually," Matt began as he chomped away on yet another slice of pizza. His fourth by Jake's count. "Those winds now are only about 120 mph. We've got a good hour until the real winds start kicking in."

"Oh," Danny said looking unimpressed. "Cool." It was then that to his side, Chopper started to whine. Danny rubbed the dog's head and neck to ease the animal's worry. "It's OK, boy," Danny said. He looked up at his guests. "He knows what's up. He knows that a storm is coming, huh? Huh, boy? What a good boy. What a smart, good boy," Danny said in a tone that one would normally talk to an infant in.

"Most animals sense storms days before they occur," Matt said plainly. "Today, I saw a raccoon just walking down the road." Matt pronounced the word as *rag-goon*. It took everything in Jake's power not to call him out on it and make fun of him. Instead, he let Matt continue his little story. "You never see rag-goons in the day light. Mostly at dusk or night time since they are nocturnal. But that rag-goon I saw today, well, he knew. He knew there was a bad storm coming. He had to find shelter." Matt finished and sipped his beer. He had a proud look on his face, as if he just told the group before him the secret to life. Jake rolled his eyes. The girls of the group seemed interested in the talk of animals though.

"Well, I haven't seen Pepper since, like an hour ago I guess," Molly said of her pet cat. "I guess she knows that there is a huge storm coming, too. She is probably hiding in her carrier or under the couch. That is her spot after all."

"Yeah," Danny said. "That is her spot. Dumb cat. I keep stepping on her there but she insists on making that *her* spot." Danny rolled his eyes and took a sip of his beer.

"Cats are very territorial," Matt said. "I went to school to be a veterinarian. The first thing they teach you about is cat behavior. Dogs are simple, but cats, each one is different and have their own little ways about life. They are fascinating animals. That is why we have cats and no dogs at our places."

"You went to school to be a vet?" Molly asked.

"Yeah," Matt said sounding tired. "I did. One semester. I didn't like it. It was lame."

"What was lame about it?" Amy inquired.

"Oh, you know," Matt said with a tired shrug. "The whole college system is set up against the student. It sucks."

"What do you mean?" Jake said. Jake was not sure if he was egging Matt on purposefully or if Jake *really* wanted to know what Matt meant. Either way, Jake knew he was in for one hell of an answer.

"It is all rigged," Matt said. "They just want your money. That is it. College is a big business, they don't care if you learn or not or if the classes are quality. They just want your money. They already got too much of mine so I quit. It is robbery. $300 for a class and then $450 for the text book for the class. It is all set up to make you fail. The illuminati made sure of it in the 60's. It is all bullshit."

Jake was pleased with the insane answer that Matt gave him. He smiled and tipped his beer at Matt.

"Hear, hear. Fuck the system," Jake said as he took a sip of his beer. It was getting warm. He finished it up so that he could get a fresh cold one.

"It is just not for me," Matt said. He looked glum and tired. He yawned and smacked his lips. "Besides, my teacher, Professor Jazmer... he is the one that really talked me out of it. In fact, that was all he did the entire semester."

"What do you mean?" Amy asked, confused.

"All the guy would do was tell us how awful it was to be a veterinarian," Matt explained. "He said that the worst thing about it wasn't the animals. He said that putting the animals down was really the best part of being a vet because owners don't know when to say good bye. So we help the pets not suffer anymore. And that was the worst part of being a veterinarian he said- the owners."

"The owners are the worst part?" Molly asked. Her voice was borderline curious and borderline livid.

"They just all think they know it all," Matt continued. "If their pet is sick they assume it was something that they ate but chances are it is something that they are inhaling in the house. People think that animals are so similar to us humans but that could not be further from the truth. Animals are animals. Humans are humans. Giving your cat Pepto-Bismol will cause it to have loose bowels and that is a *fact*. No matter what the internet says, the pink stuff isn't going to help your kitty- it's only gonna turn their guts inside out and make them keel over and die. And good riddance I say. People should have to take a test in order to own a pet. Same thing as having a kid. They should have to take a test instead of my tax dollars paying for their welfare asses." Matt sat there in his seat staring off into space. It was as if he never said anything at all.

The group all looked at each other, not knowing what to say about any of this. Jake did the only thing that felt right at that moment- he shrugged and got up from the table. "Anyone want a beer while I am up?" Jake asked.

"Yup," Danny said raising his hand.

"Sure," Molly said. She then proceeded to finish her half a beer in one gulp.

"I'm good," Melissa said. Matt continued to look off into space.

As Jake left to grab the beers, he looked at Matt and thought about how pathetic he looked. Part of Jake felt bad for Matt though. What a strange and odd life the kid must live. Everything was either caused or somehow wrapped up in some grand conspiracy. What a way to live life. Paranoid and angry. Though the more Jake thought about it, Matt was not paranoid and angry. Matt seemed to be just over all *defeated*. Matt had no hope. No drive. No dreams. And that was what made Jake feel bad for the guy. Jake knew that feeling once or twice in his life. Sometimes it felt like nothing was going right. Nothing was going as planned at all. Life made you want to just throw in the towel. But Jake also knew how to get over that feeling of defeat- you had to, no matter what, get up and try, try, try and try again. *No matter what.* Keep going.

"Matt," Jake said. "You want a beer, man?"

Matt looked up at Jake, surprised to be asked such a question. "Oh, yeah," Matt said in a daze as if he was just waking up. "Yeah, Jake, thanks."

"Any preference? We basically got all IPA's- Dog Fish Head, Six Point, and Magic Hat. Plus, we have Yuengling." Matt looked at Jake sideways.

"It is a lager," Jake explained. "Smooth, crisp, refreshing. Not as heavy as an IPA. It is good stuff."

"Cool, I will take that then," Matt said.

"You got it," Jake said with a smile. "Two Magic Hats and a Yuengling, coming right up."

CHAPTER 3
POWERLESS

Not even 20 minutes later the lights flickered and then went out. The apartment went into complete darkness.

"There goes the power, huh?" Jake said.

"Yup," Danny responded. "Oh, well." He bent over and rubbed Choppers head. "It's all good, boy. It's OK. It's OK." Chopper whined and then turned away and headed toward the couple's bedroom. "Hmm," Danny said. "Guess he just wants to go on our bed. That is *his* spot." Danny was thinking out loud. Jake nodded his head in agreement but then stopped when he realized no one could see him move his head in the pitch black.

"Uh-huh," Jake said, embarrassed at the fact he stood there nodding in the dark. "Old Chopper is smart. He will be fine."

"What type of dog is he anyways?" Matt asked. "Seems to be a lab? Maybe mixed with shepherd?"

"We really don't know," Danny said. "I found old Chopper on the side of the road. He was abandoned by assholes. The vet said he was a mutt; you are not far off breed wise. She said that she saw a mix of lab, German shepherd and possibly husky. There is no way to tell for sure, but she said he definitely has some German shepherd in him. That is the most dominate trait. That is why he is so smart." Danny took a sip of his beer and smiled. "Smart, but a scaredy cat when it comes to thunder, lightning... and I guess you can add category 5 winds to the mix now, huh?" Danny laughed.

"I'd say," Matt said unimpressed.

"Lance?" Amy called out. "Lance, where are you?" Amy shined her flash light in the living room. There sat Lance looking around scared. "Here, honey," Amy said as she got up to comfort her son. "Here is your flash light. Look at your Elmo books, now." Amy assisted her child with his flash light. It was extremely dark in the little apartment now and downright spooky especially with all the sounds clashing outside. Amy herself was getting the chills.

"Danny, help me light some of these candles," Molly requested.

"OK," Danny said. Danny and Molly lit the candles on the table. It helped with the darkness some, but it still was a little creepy for now it looked like they were involved in some satanic ritual or seance.

"Where is Lance?" Jake asked Amy. He wasn't paying attention.

"Right there," she pointed into the living room with her flash light. Jake looked over and there sat Lance with a flash light flipping through his Elmo book. "Just hanging out with his best friend, Elmo," Amy added.

"Sheesh. That kid just loves Elmo," Jake said with a smile. He admired his son from the kitchen. "Look at him. Holding the flashlight and flipping the pages like a big boy. Sheesh. I'm going to buy him ice cream once this is all over. Fucking storm."

"You're gonna buy *me* ice cream too, you know," Amy said. "And if our windows are busted in, you are going to buy me a new *house*, mister."

"Can't I just buy you new windows?" Jake asked.

"Nope," Amy said with a smile. She moved in and gave her man a kiss on the lips. It felt good and reminded Jake how much he loved Amy. Even when she was being a pain in the ass.

"There," Molly said after she finished lighting all the candles. "Done. Romantic, huh?" She glanced over at Danny.

"Yeah," Danny said and scoffed. "Nothing says romance like 14 different scented candles burning at the same time as a giant storm of death and destruction is going on outside. Who you trying to romance? The crypt keeper?"

Molly had a look of defeat on her face. "But look," she said in a hopeful tone. "I put your favorite scent right here in front of you. Old Oak Woods. That is your favorite, right?"

"Yeah," Danny said. "It is my favorite. Thanks, baby." Danny put his arm around Molly and gave her a smooch on her cheek.

"Oh, shit," Matt said as he looked down at his cell phone.

"What is it?" Melissa asked. She sounded worried.

"No Wi-Fi," Matt answered. "I can't check on my fantasy league."

"You know we are about to die, right?" Danny asked. "And you are worried about some dumb football game bullshit?"

"Last year I won three grand playing," Matt said. "So, yeah, I am worried about 'some dumb football game bullshit'."

"Three grand, huh?" Jake asked.

"Yup," Matt said with pride. "My team slaughtered. I won by 200 points. It was a landslide. This year I am already in first and I'd like to keep it that way." Matt was breathing heavy. He looked and sounded uncomfortable.

"You alright, Matt?" Melissa asked.

"I've got to use the bathroom," Matt said.

"Go for it," Danny replied.

"Where is it?" Matt said sounding almost annoyed.

"Down there," Danny said pointing to the hall. "First door on your left."

Matt got up out of his chair and made his way to the hall. Before he entered the hallway, he turned back to the group. "Should I flush?"

"Yeah, knock yourself out," Danny said. Matt continued to the bathroom. The group heard the door close and lock and Amy scoffed.

"'Should I flush?' Gross," Amy whispered into Jake's ear. "Why wouldn't he?"

"Well," Jake began. "To save water. Since the electric is out, water is going to be next. That is why they tell you to fill up your bathtubs and sinks, so that you have water. If you are gonna drink it though, you need to boil it first."

"Ohh," Amy said. Even in the dark by candle light Amy looked gorgeous. Every contour of her face was perfection. As if Bernini himself sculpted her face. For a moment, it was hard for Jake to look away, however, Lance's horrifying scream made him look elsewhere.

CHAPTER 4
THE TURNING

Jake looked over behind him to see Molly's cat Pepper attacking Lance. The cat moved in such a way that for a moment it made Jake think he was hallucinating the whole scene that was in front of him. The cat's front paws moved so quick it looked as if everything was moving in double time. Pepper hissed and shrieked as she clawed and bit the child. Lance was frozen with fear, he could not get away, he was too young to respond to such a situation. Jake noticed that there was something off about Pepper's eyes. They seemed to glow a soft red.

Lance was screaming at the top of his lungs. It was more than a scream; it was a mortal cry for help. It was a sound that after 27 months of cries and moans and laughs and coughs, Jake had never heard his son make such a noise. It scared Jake to the core of his soul. Amy screamed as well. Before Jake could react to what was happening, Pepper swiped at the child's cheek, leaving three deep gashes on the child's face. This is when Jake saw red. No, not the red from his son's face that spurted out, yes he saw that too, but his vision turned into a certain shade of crimson.

Jake leapt up off his chair and bolted towards his son. He was acting on primal instincts as he found himself perform the most righteous and accurate kick he had ever executed. The bridge of his foot found the cat's belly and Jake launched the cat up into the air. The cat slammed against the wall above Danny and Molly's couch. Pepper hit the wall hard. She crashed down upon the cushions of the couch and no sooner did Pepper hit the fabric did she pounce back up on all fours, hissing at Jake and Lance. Jake looked down at his son. His right arm was cut to ribbons. The skin was torn and hung in an unnatural fashion. It amazed and horrified Jake that a cat could inflict such wounds to a human being. That a house hold pet could cause *this* much damage. Jake clenched his teeth and balled his fists up as he stood in front of Lance, shielding him from Pepper. Jake looked at Pepper dead in the eyes. Pepper hissed and her red eyes looked at Jake as if he was Pepper's next meal.

Now, everything seemed to move in slow motion for Jake. He watched Pepper pounced towards him. Jake could see the cat's stop light red eyes get closer. He saw blood on Pepper's coat from the attack on Lance. Jake, surprising himself once again, connected a right hook to the side of Pepper's neck as the cat was in midair. The cat flew against the wall by the hallway. It landed hard on the floor and lay still. Only its belly moved, showing signs of life. Amy came up behind Jake to care for the now near hysterical Lance.

"Oh my God!" Amy screamed. "His arm! His arm! Jake!"

"I see it, I see it!" Jake said. He glanced down at his son. The amount of blood was staggering. In his peripheral, Jake could see Pepper shaking off the last blow. Pepper was now on all fours again, back arched, mouth opened, hissing at Jake and his family. Danny, Molly and Melissa sat at the kitchen table, wide eyed and mouths a gap. They were not yet able to wrap their minds around the situation at hand. And that was understandable- no one had ever seen anything like this before.

"Fuck!" Jake cried out. "Danny! A little help with your cat, please? Molly? Anyone?"

No sooner did Jake finish his sentence did Pepper run towards Amy and Lance. Amy shrieked in terror and held Lance closer to her. Before Jake could move them out of the way to deliver yet another swift kick to Pepper, Danny sprung up from his chair, beating Jake to the chase. Danny's kick was something out of a video game as the tip of his foot caught Peppers throat perfectly. The cat was launched up into the air for a second time, this time going straight up in the air, hitting its back on the ceiling with force, and then came crashing down upon the tile floor. Danny did not hesitate as he gave Pepper a soccer like kick sending the limp cat body towards the hallway. Pepper's body slid on the tile and then skidded across the hallway rug, stopping once it hit the hallway wall with a thud. The cat was still breathing but it was stunned. There was a blood trail from where it landed on the tile and streaked across the rug to where the cat now laid breathing heavy.

"Pepper!" Molly screamed out. She ran towards the cat but Danny held her back.

"Leave her, Molly!" Danny yelled. "Go get paper towels for Lance! Melissa! You help, too! Go!" Molly did not argue as she and Melissa made their way to the kitchen to get paper towels for the injured child.

Jake now held Lance and looked at Amy. "I got him. Go get towels and some water for him. I got him." Lance cried out and this made it harder for Amy to leave her son's side but she knew it was for the best. She nodded and followed the girls into the kitchen in a rush. Jake held Lance and looked at Danny. They shot each other looks of confusion and terror. What had just happened?

"Dude," Jake began. "What the flying fuck, man?"

"I have no idea, man," Danny said. "Pepper is usually so good with kids. I don't know. I am sorry. I am so sorry man."

"Me too, man," Jake said. "I kicked your cat! I *punched* your cat! What the hell is going on?"

"I dunno," Danny said. "How's the kid?" Danny moved closer and looked at Lance's arm. Even in the candle light Danny could see the damage that was done to the child's arm. He winced. "Ohh, man. Shit, that looks-" Danny was going to say bad, but Pepper never gave him the chance. The cat dug its claws into Danny's shoulder, and then bit down hard on the skin between his shoulder and neck. Danny screamed.

Danny reached behind him and grabbed Pepper and pulled her off his back. Danny dug his nails deep into the cat's midsection before slamming her down in front of himself. The cat hit the floor and no sooner jumped back up and attacked Danny's shins with its claws and mouth. Its front paws once again moved at an unholy speed.

"For fuck's sake!" Danny yelled out. "Get off of me, Pepper! Get the fuck off!" Danny kicked the cat away. Pepper landed and sprung at Danny once again. Danny had now had enough.

He began to stomp at Pepper. His heel came down on the cat's back, knocking the air out of the animal. Still, the cat tried to attack, even though it was dazed and out of breath. Danny's heel then found the base of Pepper's skull, cracking the cat's spine. Again his heel came down, this time to the side of the animal's body, collapsing a lung and breaking ribs. The final stomp found the top of Pepper's skull. Danny's weight and force broke the animal's skull as fragments of bone pierced the animal's brain which exited out of its mouth and nose. Pepper was dead, but Danny's adrenaline was maxed out and he let down a final stomp, flatfooted. Not knowing his own strength, he flattened Pepper's head so that the animal's eyes bulged out as well as its tongue. Brain matter could be seen in the candle light, oozing out of parts of the cat's crushed skull. No sooner did Danny look down and realize what he had done did Melissa, Amy and Molly all enter the room. All three froze in their place, horrified at the sight of the once majestic cat, now a pile of bloodied and smashed fur. Danny was covered in sweat and blood. He was completely out of breath.

"Pepper!" Molly shrieked. "My cat! My baby! My Pepper! What have you done, Danny?! What have you done?!"

"I'm sorry! I'm sorry! But fuck the cat, Molly!" Danny screamed. "She fucking attacked Lance! Then she attacked Jake and then *me*! Look at my back!" Danny moved to show Molly the damage her cat had inflicted. He winced doing so. It felt like a sunburn that someone smacked with a hot iron. "I'm gonna need some bandages, too. Fuck! God fucking damn it!"

Molly did not care about the wounds her boyfriend had. She was still trying to cope with what had just happened. She was still trying to come to terms with the fact that Pepper was dead. "Why?!" Molly screamed. "You didn't have to... you didn't have to kill her you know!"

"Really? Danny said. "What was I supposed to do? Offer her a cocktail and talk things out? Look at Lance! Look at what *your* cat did to him!" Danny himself looked over at Lance. The child was a bloody mess.

"Shit!" Danny cried out. "We need our first aid kit."

"Where is it?" Jake said. He handed Lance over to Amy. Amy held the boy whom was still crying. "I will get it."

"In the bathroom," Danny said. "Under the sink."

"Matt is in there though," Melissa said. Her voice was a scared whisper.

"Jesus, still? Well, go get him or something," Danny ordered. "If he is taking a shit, fine, but just make sure to get the first aid kit. It is under the sink. Go!" Danny helped Molly wrap the child's arm with paper towels. "Make sure they are wet. That way they don't stick to the kid. Oh! And Melissa! If he *is* taking a dump tell him to light a fucking match!"

"Kid can't even do that on his own I am sure," Jake said under his breath.

"What?!" Amy said in a panic.

"Nothing. Nothing," Jake responded in a whisper.

Lance was crying in pain. His forearm was ripped to shreds. His once fleshy plump toddler arms now looked like someone dipped his arm into tomato sauce. Jake comforted his wife. He could tell that it was getting hard for Amy to breathe. She was, with just cause, going into full panic mode. It probably did not help that the weather was getting worse outside now. Elliot was no longer fucking around.

Outside the winds had picked up speed and it sounded like people were outside swinging sledgehammers at the plywood on the windows. The roof sounded as if there was a party going on top of it. A violent party, one where all the patrons were stomping around in complete disregard to their downstairs neighbors. The wind whistled like a freight train. The candle light and flash lights were no longer doing the trick. They needed *light*. Jake began to panic- he thought that if his son's injury looked bad in the dark that in the light it would look like pure hell and then some. Jake's heart began to race. The wind blew, relentless and almost unnatural. The rain fell in a cruel fashion, brutal yet pure. Elliot was making the group anxious. Melissa's blood curdling scream did not help the situation out.

"Now what the fuck?!" Jake screamed out.

"Who the fuck knows?" Danny said. "If you want something done right you need to do it yourself." Danny let out a sigh. "I will go fucking find out. Jake, keep your flash light on his wound. Amy, I know this sucks but we need to keep pressure on the cuts, OK? It will help him stop bleeding. He is going to scream, cause it hurts, but it needs to be done till we can bandage him up."

Danny seemed lost in thought when Melissa screamed again, this time, she never stopped, she just screamed at the top of her lungs for help and for god to help her. The more she screamed the more it turned into a gurgling sound and then silence.

"Fuck!" Danny shouted. He got up from Lance's side and pointed his flash light down the hall as he began to make his way over to Melissa and her screams. About four steps into the hallway, away from everyone in the living room and their view, Danny stopped dead in his tracks.

Danny's beam of light found that the hallway was now a river of blood. There was blood on the walls, on the ceiling dripping down into puddled areas upon the hallway rug. Danny held his flashlight shaking with fear. He breathed heavy and under his breath he whispered, "What the fuck?" It was then that in front of him, down the hall he heard a noise. It was a wet breaking sound. It sounded like someone was breaking celery under a kitchen sink faucet. A wet clean breaking sound followed by a loud vicious crunching sound. Danny guided his flash light down the hall to where his bedroom was. There, his light found the open and dead eyes of Melissa. Her eyes opened wide with panic and fear. Her head moving like a bobble head doll on the front dashboard of a speeding car. Danny's flash light found the now red eyes of Chopper, facing downwards into Melissa's midsection. Her stomach was open and Chopper feasted upon her guts and innards. Danny covered his mouth. Vomit came up, slow and hot, but he forced it back down. The sensation burned his throat and he coughed. Chopper looked up at him with a snarl and growled. His snout was painted with the blood of Melissa. Danny kept his flash light on Chopper but felt something move to his left, in the bathroom. The door was still opened and Danny glanced in through the corner of his eyes. There he saw Matt, eyes wide open and his throat opened even wider. He too had a hole in his belly, only unlike Melissa, Matt was completely hollowed out. Chopper had eaten Matt's insides completely. Danny began to sweat. His breathing became fast and heavy. Chopper still had him in his gaze. Danny began to walk backwards, slow and steady with the flash light still on Chopper. He made it a few steps back and Chopper went back to eating what was left of Melissa's intestines.

Danny kept his light on Chopper. He continued walking backwards towards the group. He got there, still with his eyes fixated on the hallway, and whispered. "Guys. Listen. Get up. Go. To the garage. *Now*."

"Dude, what the fuck are you talking about?" Jake said. He shot up from Lance's side. He was covered in his son's blood.

Still looking at the hallway, in a whisper Danny spoke soft and slow. "Go. To the garage. Go. NOW."

"Dude," Jake was getting pissed. "The fuck are you talking about? We need to get to a hospital, man! Where the fuck is the first aid kit? Where-" It was then that the entire group heard it. Over the terrifying sound of the now 189 mph winds outside. Over the sound of the buckets of rain falling. Over the sound of tree branches crashing down to the roads below them. Even over the hysterics of Lance. They all heard Chopper's deep and sinister growl. Worst of all, thanks to Danny's flash light beam still shinning in the direction of the hallway, they all *saw* Chopper's red eyes and head peak out. The group all gasped and sprinted for the garage once they saw the dog's head, completely blood soaked as it dripped down upon the carpet.

CHAPTER 5
IN THE GARAGE

The house shook as the wind howled. Noises were coming from everywhere. Scratching and banging, dragging and scraping. A loud crack came from outside, not lightning, a tree trunk perhaps buckling and breaking from the force of the winds. A loud thump was heard. Something hit someone's car. Whatever it was, from the sound of the thump, it without a doubt left a dent. The group just barely made it into the crowded garage of Danny and Molly. Chopper was outside the door, scratching and snarling away. Lance was crying hysterically. He not only also saw Choppers appearance, but was in a world of hurt. When Jake lifted his son up to get away from Chopper, he mindlessly grabbed the child by his arms, open wounds and all. Amy and Molly both were consoling the child trying to calm him down. It was to no avail as the child wailed as if he was in competition with the wind outside. Danny was the last one in the garage and now sat with his back against the door of the garage. Every so often his body would move from the force of Chopper slamming himself against the garage door. Danny looked as if he had seen a ghost of a ghost. He was covered in sweat as he told the group a PG version of what he saw in the hallway. Amy and Molly cried. Jake stood statuesque in disbelief of the day's events. All the meanwhile, the wind howled and the rain fell as Chopper kept at the door.

"Does anyone have a flash light?" Molly asked. Her voice was nothing more than a fatigued whisper.

"No," Jake said as he huddled down next to Amy and Lance. Amy shook her head no.

"Nope," Danny said. "I've got my phone but my battery is at 27%."

"Danny!" Molly scolded. "I told you to keep it charged! You just can't stop playing those video games, can you?"

"Whatever," Danny said. He was too exhausted to fight. "The power is out anyways, so whatever. What do you want me to do? Call the president?"

"Well, shine your phone's flashlight at the garage door," Jake said. He motioned behind the group to the large metal garage door that swayed in and out as if it was breathing. "Maybe we can get the door-" Danny interrupted him. He sounded winded. Like he just completed a marathon.

"No use," Danny said. "Power's out. There is no way to open the door. No way."

"You're kidding, right?" Jake said. "There is no emergency exit or something?"

"The fuck do I look like? A garage door expert?" Danny said snapping his gaze up at Jake. "Besides, even if we had power- look! Look at this place. Look at all these fucking boxes, man. We would have to move them and we don't have the time or energy. My phone doesn't even have the energy. It is already down to 20%. Sorry, man. Sorry. I'm sorry. Molly. I'm sorry."

Jake had never seen his friend this way before. He knew things were bad. The house continued to shake. Chopper continued to rage at the door. Lance continued to wail in pain. Jake looked at his wife. They've been through a lot together. They had known each other for 10 years. Married for 8 of the 10. Accidents and illnesses happened, Amy and Jake had seen the worst side of each other. Lance was a blessing for them, but still, it was not an easy birth (is there really such a thing?). Lance was turned sideways in the womb. Their doctor made due and was able to get Lance out head first; however, the cord was around his neck. Jake saw this. He watched the birth and saw it all firsthand. He saw more than Amy saw. Truth be told, it was a tough event to witness, but also, the single best thing that Jake had ever seen. His father-in-law told him this prior to the birth of Lance.

"Watching a child being born is the most amazing thing that you will ever see in your life time," he told Jake. Jake called bullshit and cheated by watching birthing videos on YouTube. He could barely get past the first 15 seconds, he didn't even make it to the crowning, he had to turn the videos off and then watch cartoons to get the images of bloody swollen vaginas and plump sweaty thighs out of his mind. Jake was certain that the day Lance was born, he would not watch. For if he did, he would faint. There was no doubt about this in his mind. But the day came, and not only did Jake watch the birth of his son, but he watched like a champ. He was like a rock. He saw it all. His father-in-law was right- it *was* the most amazing thing that Jake had ever witnessed. Now, seeing his son, arms tore up, gashes on his cheek and forehead, Jake felt awful. He felt sick. He felt guilty and helpless. The fact that he caused more harm to his son was beginning to eat him up inside. Jake realized this and no sooner did he notice it, he squashed the emotion. He did what he had to in order to protect his family from what seemed like a rabid dog that was possessed by the devil. That was when it hit him- a strange calm came over Jake. He knelt down by his wife and child's side. All three covered in Lance's blood. He stroked his wife's back. He patted his son's head. He whispered, "I'm sorry" to them and then kissed them both, Lance first then Amy. Then he stood up and looked at his friend Danny who was still a sweating and shaking mess.

"Dude," Jake said. "Where is your gun?"

Danny's eyes shot up, they looked like two full moons on his face. "Are you kidding me?" he asked. "Why do you want to know where my gun is?"

"Umm," Jake said and pointed at the door. Chopper was still going ape shit against it, still making Danny's body jerk back and forth. "Because *that.*"

Danny scowled and then scoffed. He shook his head and wiped his brow. "I just bashed my wife's cat's head in, and now you want me to shoot my dog?"

Jake sighed and threw his hands up. "Well, either that or you give him some fucking pup-peroni. Shit, man. Yes, goddamn it, yes, we need to kill your dog. I need to get my son to the hospital."

"Well," Danny began and then just drifted off. He had a lot to say. How dare Jake suggest to simply shoot his dog? After all, Chopper was his pal, his best friend, from before he even got involved with Molly. Chopper was a good dog. A good dog that had gone bad. Danny hung his head. "My gun is out there. By the front door."

"Fuck. My. Ass," Jake said.

"We need to get Lance to a hospital, Jake," Amy said.

"I know, I know," Jake said. He looked around the garage. Boxes. Boxes everywhere. From what he could see they were labeled "Danny's toys" "Danny's CDs" Danny's Games". Danny was a pack rat that refused to grow up Jake thought. But now was not the time to cast stones. Now was the time for action.

"Danny," Jake began, calm and collective. "Weapons. Do you have *anything* in here that we can use as weapons? So, we can at least get to your gun... and then do what we need to do?" Jake's mind was racing with what was behind that door. Chopper. Possessed and pissed and still going at it. It was a miracle that door was still standing. "I gotta get Lance to the hospital, dude," Jake continued. "His arm is torn to shit, man. Come on. Help me. Please." Jake's voice was calm and sincere, but nervous and scared at the same time. The whole room felt it.

Danny sighed. He knew Jake was right. He knew what had to be done. No matter what was behind that door behind him, it certainly was no longer his dear friend Chopper. This was now a different beast all together. The pounding on the door continued. The wind outside tore through all that dared to stand in its way. The rain fell in thick long drops. Danny wiped his brow again and took a deep breath.

"OK, OK, Jake," Danny said. He took a deep breath and swallowed the air. "Well, I'm not about to get up. I think I am bracing this door with my weight. I guess being a fat ass was a blessing in disguise." Danny laughed. He laughed alone. "So, look. The only thing I have in here are tools. I've got hammers, screw drivers; I think I have a shovel back over them boxes, to the right. There is a machete and I've got a sledge hammer around here somewhere, too. Fuck if I know where that is right now. But with that shovel... We can... we can at least hold Chopper off with the shovel. You and I. The girls and Lance will need to stay here until we come back."

"And if you don't?" Molly asked. It was a grim and morbid question but honest and true. What if they did not make it? What if Chopper got the best of them both?

"Then," Danny began slow and thought as he spoke. "You're gonna have to finish what we started. We will leave you the machete there," Danny said motioning to the machete on the wall. "Jake, grab it, give it to Molly. Amy, I've got an extra hammer... I've got extra-long screw drivers, you can use them like knives, you know. I also got a bat... what do you want?"

The house rocked back and forth. The wind slammed against the garage door sounding like God's fists were punching it from outside. Meanwhile, from inside the house, Chopper continued to attack the door. The sound of the wind and rain falling outside was scary., however, the sound of Chopper slamming and scratching at the door was downright terrifying. The group was in a nightmare scenario that none of them could have ever thought up in a million years.

"Gimme the bat," Amy said as she held Lance. He was calming down but moaned from time to time. "Gimme the bat and a screw driver," Amy continued. "Just in case, right?"

"Right," Danny said. "OK. Jake, you get the shovel. I will take the hammer. It is my dog, so I think it should be me that puts him down, but you need to lead the way. You need to get that shovel out the door here and push him back. As far back as he will go. If we can do this, if we get him back towards the hallway again, then I can grab my gun and... well, end this. Then, we get the fuck outta here. We go to the hospital. Get Lance taken care of. Does this sound good to everyone? Everyone feel good about it?"

The group all nodded their heads yes. There was no time for cute responses or concerns. Lance was in trouble and Chopper still slammed his body against the door in a rage. It was go time.

"Awesome," Danny said sarcastically, he sounded drained. "Well then... let's go kill my fucking dog."

CHAPTER 6
MAN VS BEAST

Danny stood up, pressing his back against the door. As he did, he moved forward and Jake could see the door buckle- it was not going to hold much longer.

"Ready?" Danny said looking at Jake.

"Yeah," Jake said. "You?"

"As ready as I will ever be," Danny moaned

"I hear that, bro," Jake whispered.

"You guys be careful!" Molly said.

"And Jake- *hurry*, please," Amy added.

"I will, babe. Everything is going to be OK," Jake said. His tone was believable but deep inside his gut he was in full anxiety mode. Danny brought him back to reality.

"OK, Jake. Get the shovel ready. You're gonna have to push him back. Don't worry about hurting him, I think, I am sure actually, that whatever is behind this door is no longer Chopper. It is... some other beast altogether. So, don't hold back. Do what you must, bud."

"Will do," Jake said. His heart was racing. He wished he had a better weapon than a shovel. Molly's machete would be great. Or a chainsaw. Yeah, a chainsaw would be epic. Or-

"Dude," Danny said interrupting Jake's day dreaming of weapons of mass destruction. "It is go time."

Jake nodded. He looked back at Amy and blew her a kiss. Jake stood ready at the door with the shovel head aimed at the shaking door. The wind crashed against the house. The rain fell in buckets. Chopper continued his savage assault on the door.

"You ready?" Danny asked. Jake tried not to look at him, Danny seemed to be shaking and crying.

"Yeah. Let's... Yeah," Jake replied weakly.

"On three then," Danny said back. "One."

Jake grasped the shovel tight. In his mind, he was expecting a hulked out vicious dog. A dog that had uncanny strength and that only a nuke bomb could stop. But Jake did not have a nuclear bomb, he only had an old rusty shovel. It didn't matter *what* Jake had in the end for all that mattered was the simple task at hand- keep his family safe.

"Two," Danny spoke in a half whisper.

Jake felt himself begin to pour sweat. The air was thick and Jake felt like he was going to pass out. Everything seemed to move, vibrate almost. His eyes had adjusted to the dark of the garage which was a good thing, he would be able to see Chopper clearer once in the house. His plan was not to simply push the dog back so Danny could get his gun and put him down. No, Jake's plan was to inflict as much damage to the dog as he possibly could. He wanted to slow the dog down and injure it so that in the event that Chopper got by him and Danny, the girls would stand a chance against the beast. Outside, the wind and rain did their thing. Jake heard the roof shingles fall and crash to the ground. Molly gasped. Amy cried. Lance moaned. Danny yelled.

"Three!" Danny shouted, so loud it was heard over the storm.

As Danny opened the garage door to the hallway, Jake maneuvered the shovel out and into Chopper, startling the dog and forcing it to retreat backwards. Jake surprised himself at how perfect the plan was working out (so far.) All that mattered to Jake was that Chopper was away from his family- mission accomplished. Jake poked and prodded the shovel at Chopper, striking the dog in the head and snout. Danny pushed out of the door behind Jake as he drove the shovel head into Choppers neck, forcing the animal back and to lose its breath for a mere moment which was all the guys needed. Both Jake and Danny made it out of the garage; Danny slammed the door shut after him. Jake wasted no time and jerked the shovel at Chopper again, this time hitting the beast on his snout. The dog howled in pain and retreated back into the hallway. The plan was working.

"Again!" Danny cried out from behind Jake. Danny had his hands on Jake's shoulders. Jake, full of anxiety and adrenaline plunged the shovel towards Chopper a third time, only to miss the dog completely. His eyes were not used to the dark as well as he had thought they would be. The first few strikes on Chopper landed due to nothing more than luck.

"Keep at it!" Danny yelled. In his mind, Danny was tracing all his steps. He would stay behind Jake until Chopper was in the hallway, hopefully Jake would be smart enough to suppress the dog until Danny told him it was clear. This would be when Danny would have his gun, ready to fire on the beast. Danny was not concerned about wasting bullets; he had a drawer full of rounds in his bedroom closet. He was going to empty his magazine into his dog. 16 hollow point rounds ought to do the trick. Danny felt his heart race as they got closer to the hallway. He would soon be able to make his break. Jake swung the shovel up and down and struck Chopper on the side of his skull. The dog once again whined and retreated back. All the while its red eyes stared at the two friends. Chopper was far enough back into the hallway; Danny could get out from around Jake and get his gun.

"Heads up, bro!" Danny yelled. "Making my move! Cover me!"

"On it! On it!" Jake exclaimed as he swung the shovel faster at the dog.

Danny broke out from behind Jake and towards the table by the front door. He could see the gun but did not see Lance's book and stumbled over it. He crashed into the table, knocking the gun back and onto the ground out of sight.

"Shit!" Danny cried out.

Jake turned to look at his friend to see what had happened. "What? What? You OK? You have the gun? Do you have it?"

"No! I-" before Danny could finish his sentence, Chopper was on him. When Jake looked away the dog took the opportunity to strike against the prey that was not an apparent threat. Chopper bit down on Danny's left arm, the arm that held his hammer. The hammer fell from his hand as Chopper shredded Danny's arm while on top of him. They both fell back and onto the floor. Chopper snarling and biting like mad, Danny screaming for Jake to help.

"Get him off! Get him off! Holy fuck! Chopper! Get off!" Danny screamed.

To Jake, it all happened so fast, yet, it all happened in slow motion. He froze. It was terrible timing for a panic attack but some things just cannot be avoided. The first thing that came into Jake's mind was to kick the dog and so he did just that. Jake kicked Chopper as hard as he could. His foot connected with the side of Chopper's torso. Jake could feel the tip of his toes go in between the dog's ribs, there was a loud crack as Jake broke two of the dog's ribs. Chopper seemed unfazed by the strike as he stayed on top of Danny, ravaging his owner's arm.

"Hit him! Hit him!" Danny screamed out. It clicked in Jake's head now that he was holding a shovel the entire time. Jake rose his hands up with the shovel in hands and brought the shovel down on to the dogs back. Jake did not wait for a response from the dog and continued to beat the dog, slamming the shovel down on to the beast's back, over and over again. The dog was relentless and began to drag Danny back to the hallway. The pain Danny was feeling was out of this world. He could hear his skin being torn off from his arm. He could *hear* Choppers teeth touch his bone and rub against it. It was a nasty unnatural scraping sound. Danny was shocked that his dog, his precious mutt, was now dragging him to the hallway. Up until this day, Chopper had never bit anyone. Danny was hopeless and scared out of his wits. Chopper was dragging him into the hallway. Danny knew what was down that hallway. Death.

"Jake! Shoot him! Shoot him!" Danny screamed out. As Chopper dragged Danny he was able to reach out and grab his hammer. Danny now began to hit Chopper with it. He was only able to hit and connect on the dog's torso. Danny tried to hit the dog's head but it was at an odd angle for him. Danny was only grazing the dog's head with the hammer.

"Jake! Get the gun! Shoot him!" Danny yelled. "It fell behind the table! Shoot him!" It was pitch black in the room. Jake could not see the look of desperation in his friend's face, but he could hear the desperation *and* pure terror in Danny's voice.

"OK!" Jake screamed back. "I'm looking! I'm looking!" Jake stepped on the same book that Danny slipped on but was able to hold his balance. He made it to the table and on his hands and knees he searched for the gun.

"Hurry!" Danny cried out. He was moaning and out of breath. His dog was getting the best of him.

Jake continued to look for the gun. It was a simple task really-bend down, pat the ground, find the gun and kill the beast. But in the pitch dark and in a rush the task became monumental. The seconds felt like days. Danny was making awful sounds. Something was wrong. This gun hunt was taking too long. Jake had enough.

With a battle roar that the girls and Lance could hear in the garage, Jake and his shovel made their attack on Chopper. Jake brought the edge of the shovel down into the dog's spine. Over and over and over again. Jake felt hot liquid hit his arms and chest. He continued to bring the shovel up and down. Jake felt himself become exhausted but he continued until the canine fell silent. All Jake could hear was his own breathing. He tasted heavy iron on the tip of his tongue and he spat. He dropped to his knees to tend to Danny.

Jake rolled the corpse of Chopper off of Danny. "Danny! Danny! What the fuck, man? Danny!" Jake repeated over and over. There was a tiny gargle and what Jake made out to be Danny's last breath. Jake could not see anything in the candle light. He looked behind him. The door. The door was right there. He could open the door quick and see for a moment. So, it may get wet and windy. So what? He had to help Danny. Jake got up to his feet and opened the door to the outside world. The wind took full advantage of this opportunity and swung the door wide open. The rain followed and soaked Jake's shoes and pants. He did not care. He turned around to tend to his friend and that was when he realized he was too late.

There laid his best friend, Danny, Daniel Robert Murphy, dead in a pool of blood. Danny's throat was torn wide open. The white of his larynx could be seen as well as the brownish white of his spine. Chopper killed his master. Jake walked over to the body. Danny's eyes were still open, as was his mouth. Danny had a horrified look on his face. Jake couldn't bear to look at it. He found a blanket on the couch and placed it over his friend's body. Some of the blanket covered dear old Chopper too. Jake teared up at the sight of Chopper as he and his shovel really did a number to the beast. Jake tucked the blanket in under his best friend and his dog. He especially did not want the girls to see the state that they were in. *Jake* did not want to see the state that they were in.

The wind was beginning to become too much. The rain was no big deal but the wind was like nothing Jake had ever felt or seen before. He looked down at Danny and Chopper and made sure that the blanket covering them was secure. It was. He then looked over at the kitchen table and saw the flash lights. It took some, effort but Jake closed the door. Before the door shut, he saw what appeared to be road flares out in the streets. Some were in the bushes too which he found odd but chalked it up to the fact the winds more than likely blew the flares all about.

Jake finally got the door closed. It was quiet in the little condo. It was also now completely pitch black as well. The wind blew out all the candles in the kitchen and now the wind seemed to laugh at Jake from outside the door. Howling laughter. Jake sneered as he walked with care to the kitchen. He reached into the darkness and found a flash light. He turned it on and looked at Danny and Chopper yet again just to be sure they were hidden from the girls' view. They were. He knew this, he was certain. He did a damn good job of tucking the blanket in under the bodies. Jake poked the bodies with his shovel head. He just wanted to make sure that the dead bodies were indeed still dead and that this wasn't some cheesy 80's film were the dead return to life. No, lucky for Jake in this case, the dead remained dead. Danny was still dead. Chopper was still dead. Pepper was still dead. Melissa and Matt, they were still dead as well. Melissa and Matt. *Damn*, Jake thought. *I can't believe that they are dead, too.* Reality was hitting Jake. He found that it was a tough pill to swallow. He shook his head to clear his mind. *First aid kit* he thought. *I need to get the first aid kit. I gotta patch Lance up. Some good just may come out of all of this after all.* Jake took a deep breath and with his flash light made his way into the hallway.

At first, Jake could not believe his eyes. In fact, he laughed at the sight that was down the hallway and in the bathroom. Whereas his friend Danny was gripped with horror by the same sight, Jake could only laugh. Jake understood the reality that was before him. He knew this was not a joke. But it was just too much for him to take. It was too surreal. It was an all-out horror show. The day's events were something that you would only read about or see in the movies. Fiction. This was all fiction. A board game. The game Clue, came to mind. Or those old What if...? games. What if you had to go without sight or hearing? Which would you choose? What if you had to give up the internet for a month and in return you would get a million dollars? Could you do it? What if your house hold pets started attacking you? What would you do? Well? What *would you do* if it happened to you? There is no answer. No one thinks about these things. No one thinks that they will ever really happen. What if...?

Jake stood in the hallway, laughing with tears in his eyes. The sight of Matt, hollowed out and neck tore open, the sight of his cousin, a human being that he watched grow since birth, laying in a puddle, no, more like a *lake* of her own blood. Her throat open, stomach open, eyes open- this all had to be a joke. A prank. A goof. There was no way this was real. And so Jake laughed. This was his defense mechanism kicking in. He *had* to laugh. *He had to.* Otherwise, once he found Danny's gun, he would be inclined to put the barrel into his mouth, pull the trigger, and pierce his brain with a bullet.

So Jake laughed. He smiled and his eyes teared up. The scene before him was gruesome and macabre but he was doing OK. He was breathing. His heart was beating. Blood was pumping. He was alive. He was holding up just fine. Everything was going well in his head until it occurred to him *why* he was in the hallway. He was standing there because he meant to get the first aid kit for his son. His son that had an arm that was torn to ribbons courtesy of a cat named Pepper. Instead, he locked eyes with the corpses of the once love birds. The laughing stopped and reality hit, and it hit hard. Danny was dead. Matt was dead. Melissa was dead. Lance, Jake's son, his own flesh and blood, was seriously injured. There was a category 5 hurricane outside. Jake, his son, his wife and Danny's girlfriend, Molly, had to go out into the storm in order to get to the hospital. Once they did, the doctors would stitch Lance up and he'd be OK. The storm would be over in a day, maybe two when considering the outer rims of the storm. Then, clean up. The streets. All the branches. The debris. The idiotic "Vote For" signs that once littered the sides of the roadways, all blown away to hell and back. Clean up. Clean up and then three funerals. Five if you included Pepper and Chopper. What a fucking nightmare. Jake shook his head and made his way into the bathroom. He refused to make eye contact with Matt again. He opened the cabinet beneath the sink and began to rummage through. His flash light revealed a box of tampons, hair products, razors for the shower, shampoo, towels and finally the first aid kit. It was still in its cellophane wrapping. Jake took the first aid pack out and made his way out of the bathroom. Not once did he ever look back into the dead eyes of Matt or Melissa. Jake did not want to remember them that way.

CHAPTER 7
MAN VS NATURE

Jake stood at the foot of the hallway, holding the flash light and looking at the front door. The wind was worse than before. Howling and slamming rain and dead parts of nature at the house. It sounded like an awesome party was going on and Jake was too exhausted to participate. Too tired care. He blinked his eyes and swallowed hard. He was thirsty. He should drink something. He stared at the door with intensity. He couldn't look away. There was scratching at the door. Twigs or fallen branches perhaps? Maybe even glass from a car window? Maybe it was the devil himself trying to get into the house for shelter?

Jake squinted his eyes and whispered to the door. "Fuck you," he said in a gentle tone. "Fuck this." Jake walked over to the table and shined the flash light around it. He moved the table out some and there was a thud. Danny's gun fell as it was leaned up against the table and wall. Jake bent over and examined the piece of machine. It was a gun, but at that moment it was something more. It was Danny's gun, and somehow Jake felt a connection between it and his dead friend. Jake felt a touch of hope. He did not know why. It was not like he could use the gun now. Chopper was dead. A gun is about as useful as a paintbrush against a hurricane. But still, Jake felt better. He felt hope and ready for whatever may come next.

"Danny? Jake?" a soft voice said from the direction of the garage. It was Molly. "Is it... is it safe? Hello?"

Jake sighed and gripped the gun harder. Molly. Jake now had to tell Molly what had happened and more so that her love, Jake's best friend, was dead. Jake shook his head and walked to the garage door. He peaked at the remains of Danny and Chopper. They were still covered. Jake was somewhat relieved but that was just half the battle.

"Hey," Jake said in a soft voice as he approached Molly at the door. He shined his flashlight at her. She had her head out the door and that was about it. She squinted at the light. Her face looked like an angel to Jake, he hated that he had to tell her-

"Where...where is Danny?" Molly asked. "Is he OK?" Jake shook his head no. Fuck. He wanted to do more than just shake his head. Molly continued. "Is he... is he... did he?" Jake felt himself getting choked up as he continued to just stand there in front of Molly shaking his head. His tears solidified Molly's fears.

"How?" she cried out. "What... what happened?"

"Fucking Chopper," was all Jake was able to get out as he sobbed.

"Is it safe...?" Molly asked through her waterfall of tears.

"Yeah," Jake said. The words barely left his lips and Molly burst through the door. Jake grabbed her wrist as she came by him. "Don't," he said.

"Don't what?" Molly asked. Jake looked at her. Her eyes were wide with panic and woe. Tears streamed down her face.

"Don't... don't look," Jake said. "Just let them be."

"What...? Why? Get off me!" Molly said. She broke away and stood over the blanket covered corpses of Danny and Chopper.

"Don't... don't take the blanket off. Please," Jake begged. "Please leave it. And...don't go to the bathroom or hallway. Melissa and Matt..." Jake trailed off. Visions of his cousin and boyfriend opened up dead in pools of blood crashed into his mind. He did not laugh like before. Instead, he swallowed the vomit that rose up from his belly. "I didn't... I didn't get a chance to cover them yet." Jake said. He heard a moan from the garage and that brought him back to mission that he was on. He had to tend to his son and wife. He left Molly alone in the living room to mourn her losses. If she moved the blanket, fuck it, it was on her. He warned her. He had bigger fish to fry. Whales.

"Oh my God. Jake!" Amy cried out. He could see her eyes full of tears. Face full of sweat. "What happened?"

Jake knelt down and rubbed Lances head. The boy was sucking his thumb. He did not look up at Jake. Jake still smiled and then looked at Amy. His smile faded as he opened the first aid kit. "Danny is dead. Chopper killed him. I killed Chopper, I was too late to save Danny. Melissa and Matt, they are dead too. Chopper..." more images of open throats and tossed guts in the hallway and bathroom. Jake fell silent as Amy began to cry.

"Oh my God. Jake. I am so sorry," she said. Jake sniffled with her and nodded his head as acceptance of her remorse. "Chopper... he is such a good boy though. I don't understand?"

"I dunno," Jake said. "He *was* a good boy. I don't know what happened. Here, I got him," Jake said reaching for Lance. "I will start bandaging him up. Go check on Molly. Make sure she doesn't move the blanket, Amy. It is... It's not pretty what is underneath. Trust me."

"OK," Amy said. It was more a question than a statement response.

"Don't go down the hallway either," Jake said. "Melissa and Matt... I didn't get to cover them up. So... don't go down that way." *Throats. Guts. Blood. Open eyes.*

"OK," Amy said. This time it was a stern understanding of what Jake was saying.

"And Amy," Jake said. "I love you."

"I love you," Amy said. She gave Jake a kiss and then got up to make her way to Molly. Jake watched his wife enter the darkness of the hallway. His heart raced. It was as if it was the first time he had ever seen her. He smiled a tearful smile. Lance moaned, bringing Jake back again to reality.

Jake shined the flash light on Lance. Jake shook his head with a frown. Lance's arm was a disgusting mess. It looked worse now that Jake was really looking at the wounds. Under the crude light that came from the flash light Jake saw the deep gashes and bright red blood. Much different than the blood of Danny, Melissa, Matt and even Chopper. All of their blood was a deep dark red. Syrupy. Almost black. Lance's blood was like fruit punch. Jake examined his son's arm before doing anything. Lance had countless cuts that were bleeding still. Dog hair and cat hair stuck to the wounds. The top of the child's hand was open from Pepper's vicious bites. Jake could see the bones of his son's hand. It was something no father should have ever bear witness to. Jake felt lightheaded. He realized he still had to *clean* his son's injuries before he wrapped them up. As he thought about what he had to do next, he began to feel ill. His stomach turned with the thought of Lance screaming in *further* agony. Lance was a tough little dude but there is a limit to everyone's pain threshold. There was no way Jake was going to be able to do this by himself.

"Amy?" he called out. Jake felt bad interrupting Molly's moment of grief but what could he do? He raised his voice so the girls could hear him over the wind and rain that still pounded against the building. "Molly? I'm... I'm gonna need your girl's help. Please. We need to bandage Lance up. I need help. The-" Jake stopped as the girls both entered the garage. They stood arm in arm, Molly leaning her head on Amy's shoulder. They both looked like ghosts to Jake. Pale complexions and their faces were sunken in from crying. Jake continued on in his normal volume voice.

"The peroxide," he said. "We need to clean the wounds and ... it is gonna sting the kid like a bitch. We may need to... you may have to hold him down."

The girls looked at each other and they both nodded that they understood.

"I will be as quick as possible," Jake said. "I will clean his wounds, wrap him up and then we need to get to the hospital. We need to..." Jake thought about his next words as they sounded crazy to even himself. He couldn't imagine how they would sound to the girls. "We need to leave."

"We can't go outside...!" Molly said. She was pale. Flush. Panicked. "Just, we- we just need to call 911. They will come and get-" Jake interrupted her hysterics.

"Phone lines are down, no signal," Jake said as he held up his cell phone. "We need to get Lance to a hospital, *now*. You can stay here! I don't care. Once we get him bandaged up, I am going. I am taking Lance to the hospital."

"So am I!" Amy said. "I'm coming with you!" She had tears in her eyes and Jake felt bad. He assumed that Amy knew she was coming with them. She was the boy's mother after all, and his wife. There was no one on earth he rather have by his side. Amy was Jake's everything.

"Of course, babe, of course," Jake said. "But first. We gotta... we gotta do this."

Amy nodded with a face full of tears and sweat. The hurricane outside raged on as the big metal garage door behind them shook and rattled. Both Amy and Molly looked terrified. Jake snickered.

"Don't worry about the wind," he said. "If something was gonna happen, it would have already. Let's just do this so we can get the hell out of here, OK?" Jake's little speech brought both the girls back to reality. Amy knelt behind Lance, holding him and shushing him as she touched his neck and head.

"Where do you want me?" Molly asked.

Jake took a deep breath and assessed the situation. "Well," he said. "I think it would be best if you held his legs, just in case he starts to kick. Also, sit beside me in case I need you to help with bandages and tape." He held up the materials he was going to be using.

"OK," Jake said holding up the peroxide bottle. "First thing is first and this is going to be hell. I am going to pour this on his arm, then with these gauzes here clean out the wounds the best I can. Amy- you just comfort-" he was interrupted by an anxious Amy.

"I know what to do, Jake," Amy said. "Just get to it. We need to get out of here."

Jake pressed his lips together and nodded his head. "Of course. OK, then. Here we go." Jake looked at Lances face. He was still sucking his thumb and staring off into space. "Sorry, champ," Jake said. "Daddy loves you."

Jake took his son's arm, gentle, as if Lance's arm would fall off if Jake was any rougher. Looking at Lance's arm, there was almost a chance of it. It was torn to shreds. Deep but clean lacerations. The blood had slowed to a trickle now. Jake was thankful for this. It meant his son was not going to bleed out.

Jake uncapped the peroxide. With one hand he held the flashlight. With the other, Jake stretched Lance's arm out. It was a horror show and the sight of it made Jake's heart sink. "Here we go," he said as he poured the liquid on top of Lance's hand. The liquid hit the skin and bubbled and popped. To say Lance screamed would insinuate the pain was bearable. Lance did not scream. His eyes grew wider and wider as Jake went up and down his arm drenching it with peroxide. Lance began to shake and then let out a mighty cry, as if he was being tortured, as if he was being set on fire alive. To a child of barely three years old, the worst pain he had felt up until now was his teething experience. This pain was new and extreme. Jake grimaced as he saw his son in such discomfort. Amy cried and tried her best to soothe her son. Molly could only watch and hold down Lance's legs. He was moving them as if he was running in place. Jake could only tell his son that he was sorry over and over and over again. Jake's voice was now not only in competition with the storm outside, banging against the aluminum garage door and the buckets of rain that smashed unto the roof, but also the popping and sizzling of the peroxide as it did its job. Jake could see bits of dirt and grime come to the surface of the cuts.

"Molly," Jake said. "Hand me the gauze and hold his arm straight out. The worst is over with." Molly followed Jake's instructions. Jake dabbed the wounds with the gauze, cleaning them as he blew on them as well to give Lance that more comfort. It was what his mother and father did to Jake when he was a child. He remembered it helped him settle down. The trick was working on Lance just as it did on Jake all those years ago.

"Good, Lance, good," Jake said. "You are a strong, brave boy. Like Captain America. Or maybe you are Iron Man? Are you Iron Man?" Jake was hoping for some sort of positive reaction or at least some eye contact from his son. He received neither.

"OK," Jake said now addressing the girls. "I am going to wrap him up. Then, that is it. We are gone. We are outta here."

Molly held a tight but comfortable grip on Lance's arm. Jake began to bandage his son's arm up, making the boy's one arm look like something from an old mummy movie. Jake was more than generous with the bandages. He may have over done it but the adrenaline and anxiety of the day had taken its toll on Jake. He continued to wrap the arm so now it looked like a cast.

"I think that is good, babe," Amy said. "Just, just tape it up now."

Jake nodded in agreement. He took the tape out and taped up the bandages. Lance laid in his mother's arms, breathing heavy through tears and the sting of his peroxide soaked arm. Jake relaxed and Molly followed his lead, releasing Lance's arm down nice and slow. She rubbed his little legs. "Good job, Lance! Good job! You were so brave!" Molly said. Her smile was wide but worrisome as the storm began to whip up now in a frenzy like never before. Jake looked over at her and knew she did not want to venture outside. Truth be told, neither did he but his child's health was his number one priority. They had to get him to the hospital. Also- Jake did *not* want to be cooped up in a house full of corpses.

"OK," Jake said. He took a deep breath. "Hospital is like, fuck, a few miles. Might seem longer in this weather, but we still need to be careful. I will drive. You two," he was pointing to his family, "get in the back. Molly, if you are coming, great. We'd love for you to come. If you do, you need to sit shot gun, OK?"

"I'm gonna-," Molly stopped talking and thought for a moment. "OK. I'm coming with. But I am taking my machete."

"Awesome, fine," Jake said. "Not a bad idea. No clue what is going on out there. We actually may need it to cut branches or some shit. I've got the gun; I will take the shovel too. Fuck it. Can't hurt, right?"

The girls looked at each other and then they looked at Jake as they nodded. "OK, cool, then," Jake said. The wind howled outside. The rain could be heard as it pounded down on the ground. Jake was exhausted. The week had been trying and the last 2 hours were more than he could bear. But for his family, for his son, he would do it all over again while being set on fire. He just wanted his family to be safe.

"OK," Jake said. "I'll get the keys on the way out, they are in the kitchen. Molly, don't forget yours. We ready to do this?"

"Yes, yes," Amy said. Dumb question Jake. Amy has been ready since the very first scratch Lance received.

"Yeah," Molly said. "But, I gotta pee..."

"Well," Jake said while he was thinking. "Use the kitchen sink or trash can. Matt-" *throat open, guts eaten, eyes wide open,* "Matt is in the bathroom. You do not want to see that, Molly. And Melissa-" *laid out on the ground. Eyes like dolls. Throat torn to shreds. Belly emptied out* "is right in front of your bedroom. You don't want to see that either. So either hold it or go in the kitchen sink or trash. We are not about to judge you."

Molly thought it over for a second. Then she hung her head and frowned. "I can't hold it," she said. "So, I guess the kitchen sink it is. But... will you guys come out there with me? I... I don't want to go alone. I don't want to be alone out there with-" Molly trailed off.

"Yes," Jake said. "We will wait on the couch. That way you have privacy and are not alone. Win win. Then- we leave OK?"

Molly nodded her head up and down and wiped her nose. She was crying. "OK," she whispered. "Then we leave."

"Yup," Jake said as he stood up. "Here, let me-" he motioned to Amy and Lance so that he could hold his son, give his wife a break and he could help her up at the same time. Jake took Lance into his arms. The boy was limp. He could feel his son's breath against his neck. *Either he is in shock or he is exhausted* Jake thought. *Or maybe both.* Jake held his son tight and kissed him on the neck. A moment of peace in a time of turmoil.

"I got it," Amy said as she helped herself up. She wiped her pants off of the garage dust and dirt and the three made their way to the kitchen and couch. They walked slowly, as if not to wake the dead.

Molly made her way to the kitchen as Jake and his family sat on the couch. The wind whipped and howled like a man that had just stubbed his toe on a nail. The rain sounded like a drum machine for a heavy metal band, it pitter pattered at a violent tempo making Jake second guess himself about leaving the confines of the home. His eyes found the blanket covered corpses of Danny and Chopper and his mindset changed- he had to get out of there. He had to get his family out. More so, he had to get Lance to the hospital. Jake's mind went North and South thinking about all the scenarios that could unfold while the group headed to the hospital. The roads could be flooded, forcing them to either wait in the car or walk in waist high water. A tree could fall and smash their car. The car's window could break as they drove to the hospital. Hell, they could already be broken and they would all be sitting on broken glass with no protection what so ever from the elements. Or, everything would work out fine. The roads would be drivable. The winds would ease down. The rain would fall but nothing more than a normal South Florida rain storm. Everything would be alright. Everything was *going to be* alright. Jake looked at Amy for reassurance. She had her eyes closed and head back. Her hair was soaked with sweat. She was flushed and pale. She looked like she just got back from a night out dancing.

"OK," Molly said as she entered the living room. Amy opened her eyes and gave a tired little smile. "Done," Molly continued.

"Wiping with paper towels... that was... weird. But I feel better. Here." Molly gave Jake and Amy water bottles. "Drink up. You will feel better. I finished mine once I was done peeing. I feel... better." For the situation they were all in, Molly was positive and it was a welcomed attitude.

"Thanks," Amy said. "Jake?" She handed the bottle over to Jake so that he could open it. He did and handed back to her. He then opened his own and both Amy and Jake chugged the water as if they were in a drinking competition. Amy gave out first. Jake drank nearly the entire bottle. "That's delicious," he said as he put the bottle down in between his legs. "Water. It is amazing how great water can taste sometimes." The rain fell hard on the roof as if it was agreeing with Jake.

Jake finished his water and looked at the girls and his son. Everyone looked like the ending of a horror movie. Drained of life, but survivors nevertheless. Jake was proud of everyone in the room. This included the dead body of Danny. Danny and Jake really kicked some ass today. They actually made a difference and saved lives... well, some lives. Jake decided it was best not to think about that anymore and get a move on. He got up from the couch.

CHAPTER 8
BLOW UP THE OUTSIDE WORLD

"Everyone ready then?" Jake asked.

"Yeah," Amy said. "Let's just go. There is no sense in waiting for the wind or rain to let up. We are going to get wet regardless so, let's just go." Amy was now standing up with Lance in her arms. She was walking towards the door.

"OK, babe," Jake said. "But hang on, hang on. Molly? You still coming with us?"

"Yeah," Molly said. She looked down at Danny and Chopper. Then she looked over at where Pepper was laying. "Yeah, I am ready."

"Great," Jake said. He felt his pants for the gun and the car keys. "OK. I got the gun and the keys. Molly, you got yours?"

"Yeah," Molly said as she reached onto the table and got her house keys.

"Awesome," Jake said. He grabbed his shovel and took a deep breath. Jake walked over to the front door. The ground was slippery from when he opened the door to see Danny and Chopper. He grabbed a blanket and put it on the floor to dry up some of the water, then he kicked it to the side.

"Just be careful here, it is still a little slippery," Jake said. He put his hand on the door knob. "Amy- you go first. I will unlock the car doors. I will be right behind you." He looked at the girls and touched Lance's head. It was soaked with sweat and blood. Jake imagined it was also soaked with Amy's tears. "Keep your head down, *walk,* don't run. We don't need anyone slipping and getting hurt. Walk. OK?"

The girls both nodded. They looked more than nervous. They looked like they were going to crap their panties.

"Right on," Jake said. "Here it goes." His hand twisted the knob on the door. It was free; he could feel the wind push at the door, wanting to get in. Jake let it have its wish, and the door blew open. Amy rushed out of the door, Jake was right behind her and Molly followed. The wind blew harder than Jake expected. It hurt his skin as it pushed the stinging cold rain in his eyes. Jake blinked and wiped his brow and eyes. All he could see was Amy in front of him with Lance and the road flares… It was then that a dominating fear and regret gripped Jake.

It wasn't the mixture of the pounding rain and violent wind that made Jake regret his decision to ever leave Danny (rest in peace) and Molly's house. No, it was what happened next. The unthinkable. The unimaginable. As Amy ran with Lance in her arms in front of Jake, Jake scoped out their surroundings. He saw what seemed to be 100s of road flares lit around the apartment complex. They *looked* like road flares… but not just single road flares… *pairs.* Jake saw sets of road flares. And they were *moving.* They were closing in. They were getting closer. And that was when it clicked. That was when Jake regretted ever leaving the home. For what could be worse than running to your car in a category 5 hurricane? Well, how about the fact that those 100 plus "road flares" were actually the eyes of dogs, cats, possum, and raccoons? That same glow that Pepper and Chopper had in their eyes were also in these animal's eyes. These animals, standing out in the storm. Hunkering down somehow in plain sight, their 9 pound, 15 pound, 50 pound frames stood unflinchingly against 180 mph winds and torrential rains, as if there was no rain or wind at all. These animals stood, wet, watching and waiting. They began to, hiss and growl.

"Fuck! Fuck! Fuck!" Molly screamed out from behind Jake. He turned and his fears were realized. There he saw Molly, swinging her machete at three cats, a dog and a raccoon. The raccoon was on its hind legs, its front paws scratching and clawing at Molly. Jake could not hear them but he could see the cats hissing at Molly. The dog, a mutt of some kind, no more than 35 pounds snarled at Molly. He was in her blind spot.

"Fuck!" Jake yelled out. He considered using the gun but he couldn't get a clear shot. Instead he opted to use his trusty shovel. He swung fast and with fury; he caved in the skull of the dog, disemboweled the raccoon and broke open the cat's heads.

"Fucking run!" Jake screamed at Molly. He looked up ahead and he could barely see Amy and Lance. He only saw their silhouettes. He also saw the red eyes creeping closer towards the two silhouettes.

"Fuck, no," Jake said as he began to run towards Amy and Lance. As he got closer a raccoon jumped out at him and he knocked it away with the butt of the shovel.

In front of him stood another creature. Jake had to blink his eyes a few times to believe this but sure enough, there was a snarling red fox in front of him. From behind him, Molly sped up and she swung her machete blade down on the fox, hitting it on top of its head, breaking its skull and slicing into its brain. The fox fell into a puddle, dead.

"Holy fuck!" Jake said. He looked at Molly with wide eyes full of terror. She looked back at him with eyes full of terror and dread. Jake saw her make a motion with her hand as she tried to get the words out of her mouth. She was too slow, as the golden retriever that was now gnawing on Jake's arm had been too quick. The pain was unreal. Jake had his fill of injuries in his years. All the other injuries in his time were straight forward, clean breaks and simple gashes. This pain was a horror show. He *felt* his skin and meat being pierced and pulled off his body. The dog's paws had nails that scraped Jake on his side and neck. The pain level was high and spectacular. Jake wanted to drown himself in Jack Daniels, close his eyes, curl up, and then die.

As the dog made its first initial attack, Molly wasted no time and began to hack away at the animal as it hung on Jake's arm. She connected some amazing swings against the dog's torso but still it held its grip. It lashed all around and growled. The pain was now numbing yet it burned all the same. Jake had had enough. The pain was excruciating but more so, his son had to get to the hospital. Play time was over.

"Back up!" Jake screamed at Molly. "Move! Move! Get the fuck out of the way!" Molly moved as Jake reached for the gun, put it to the dog's head, point blank, and fired. The sound was huge. Even over the rain and winds, the shot rang out and froze all of the other red eyed beasts that laid in wait. The dog fell to the wet ground into a puddle of water. Jake kicked the corpse of the dog and looked up at Molly.

"Come on!" Jake said as he motioned to Amy and Lance. Molly, scared out of her wits but holding it together, nodded. She gulped and was ready for whatever else was going to happen. It was then that Amy cried out in pain.

There was a dog, latched on to and gnarling away at Amy's leg. On her back, two cats clawed and hissed. What looked like an otter (an *otter!*) was biting Lance's foot. Luckily, the child still had his shoes on but he screamed in terror nevertheless. Amy tried to move forward but it looked as if the dog was biting her knee. Amy held on to Lance with all of her might. Both mother and son screamed out in pain and in fear.

Jake wasted no time as his shovel found the otter and almost cut the rabid creature in two. The otter fell dead to the ground but Jake still stomped on its skull to make certain. Molly swung wildly at the dog until it stopped moving and let Amy out of its grip. Jake used the handle of the shovel to get the cats off Amy's back. Amy fell to her knees. The pain was overwhelming. She held Lance and cried. It was hard to hear her moans over the wind as it blew harder than ever before. Jake crushed and smashed the two cats with his shovel. As he leaned over to help Amy up, Jake felt the eyes of the beasts close in. They were hunched down, stalking their prey. Cats, dogs, raccoons, a fox, possum and even a skunk, all red eyed, all staring the small group down.

Jake looked to his right, the car was right there. Only two parking spots away. Jake walked forward and opened the car via remote. The lights went off signaling that the car was now unlocked.

"Come on!" Jake yelled out. "The car! It is right there! It is right-" Jake turned to look at Amy and Lance and he froze at the sight that was before him. Amy was on the floor, what looked like a pit bull ate away at her face. Lance was lying to the side of Amy, somehow unharmed other than his previous wounds. Jake wanted to yell his wife's name, but he knew that it was too late- she was gone. He frowned. He took out the gun and fired three shots into the animal's skull. It fell on the corpse of his wife. Molly swooped in and grabbed Lance. The child was alive but limp. She got right into Jake's face and with fire in her eyes she yelled at him. He saw her mouth move. Felt her breath on his face. Saw the concern in her brow. But

Jake heard nothing. He was dazed. Molly yelled again. This time, Jake heard her loud and clear.

"Jake! Let's fucking go! Go! Get in the car! Get in the fucking car!"

Jake snapped out of it and it was perfect timing. A little 20-pound mutt of some sort lunged at Jake's ankle. It was about to make contact when Jake shot the animal in between the eyes. The sound of the gun scared the animals, but they soon regrouped and once again they surrounded Jake, Lance and Molly. By this time though, Molly already had Lance in the back seat of the car and Jake had his hand on the handle to enter the car. He fired another shot up into the air, hoping to buy some more time by scaring the beasts. It worked. They froze in their steps. Jake wasted no time and opened the car door. He got in, slammed the door shut and turned only to see Molly fighting for her life as a German shepherd grabbed her arm. The weight of the dog pulled her out of the car and down on to the wet ground. Jake was not able to say anything other than "Molly!" As she fell back she gave him a look. A look that was void of all hope. As she fell back, Molly slammed the car door shut, saving Jake from the sight of her being consumed by the beasts.

Jake sat in the car for a moment with Lance in the back seat. Other than Hurricane Elliot, it was silent. The wind was loud as a freight train and the rain fell like fists upon the car's roof and windshield. Jake blinked his eyes, trying to grasp all of the events that had just unfolded. His wife, his best friend, his cousin, and her boyfriend, all dead in less than an hour. Now, Molly. Molly's death stood out in his mind the most. She was putting Lance in the car. Making sure he was safe. Her eyes were strong, her face, confident and calm. Even when the dog latched on to her, there was no panic in her face. There was only acceptance. There was peace. Jake began to weep.

CHAPTER 9
GONE WITH THE WIND

After securing Lance and making sure he was as good as he could be, Jake drove down the street. His arm was bleeding from the dog bite but lucky for Jake, it only hurt when he looked at the wound. Lance sat in the back seat. Buckled in and crying. The wind blew. The rain fell. The red eyes watched. They followed them. The car's wipers were on high and still the only thing Jake could see was the red eyes of dogs, cats, possum, and raccoons. They lined the road, as if the lone car was their own private parade. As if they were cheering them on to make it to the hospital. Jake gripped the wheel tight. He clenched the gun and drove slow. He looked every last animal straight in their dead red eyes. Lance sobbed in the back. He cried for his mother. He cried for Aunt Molly. Aunt Melly. Repeat. Jake was getting tired. He shook his head to wake himself up.

"We got this, bud," Jake said. "Don't you worry. Don't you cry, little man. We got this." Jake looked at the car's speed. They were crawling at barely 7 miles per hour. He looked in the back seat. Lance was fighting sleep... or was he fighting death? "Stay with me, bud," Jake said. "Stay with me, Lance. Come on, we got this. We are almost there. Almost at the hospital. Daddy will keep you safe."

Jake looked out his window. It was a mess. It was hell on earth. All the beasts of the earth devouring people and weaker sub species. Jake watched in horror as two dogs, a boxer and an English bulldog tore into an iguana, eating it alive as the reptile clawed at the bulldog's face. Jake saw a woman, overweight and mid aged, covered in cats that scratched her and bit her face. She would throw them off of her only to have them land on their feet and pounce right back on her. She would go on to trip over a fallen branch, only to be covered by felines and then feasted upon. A cop, dead for who knows how long, was now nothing more than but a meal for an entire family of possum. There was chaos all around as Jake drove through the abyss of hell, unnoticed for the time being.

The wind picked up, howling sounds of terror as it shook the car. The rain fell as if the car had suddenly gone under a waterfall. The windshield wipers were all but useless, Jake couldn't see anything. Nothing but big drops of water as the rain hit the windows and covered the car, street, city and state completely. "Water, water, everywhere..." Jake said with a chuckle. Jake looked behind him to check on Lance. He was awake. He was groggy and exhausted, but he was awake and *alive*.

Jake looked past his son and out the back window. Red eyes for as far back as Jake could see. Even in the storm, they were there. Jake turned forward and in the distance in front of them, a building with flickering lights. The flickering lights of Jackson Memorial Hospital. In front of the hospital and all around the car, the red eyes watched. Despite the wind, rain and debris, they watched. And they followed. And soon, they would feed.

-THE END-

The Last Meal of George Mills

Dedicated to the future-
May it always be full of hope and love.

CHAPTER 1
TURKEY DELUXE

They said that the end of the world was supposed to happen on Dec 12th, 2012. For Mr. George Mills, this statement was indeed true. December 12th, 2012 was the day that George lost his wife Paulette to breast cancer and life as he knew it was over.

George met Paulette in High School. He was a senior and she a freshman. To say it was love at first sight would be an insult to what it really was- two lost souls meeting together once again after what seemed like years, possibly eons, of being apart. The two were inseparable. Even when George shipped out to the war, Paulette wrote him every week. Those letters proved to be George's saving grace. In fact, George swears that it was her letters that helped him survive the war. Somehow, even when he was face down in the rice paddies, hot iron flying in every which direction, the thought of Paulette kept him full of hope and love. Face down in the mud, somehow, he could still smell her scent. That phantom flowery sweet smell, it kept George going. It kept him fighting. And to Paulette, George was her knight in shining armor. The most handsome man she had ever laid eyes upon. George was kind, gentle and strong. He remained that way up until the day that she passed away. Then, things changed inside of George. His life was turned upside down. He had seen and been through more than most. Being a Vietnam veteran, George was no stranger to death. Even prior to the war, George had dealt with the loss of friends and family. With no kids of his own, George was the last of his bloodline.

After the war, he and Paulette tied the knot and settled down on Herbert Avenue in Valley Brook. It was a nice home. A two story, 3 bedroom 1.5 bathroom. A finished basement that he made his wood shop where he would fiddle. His wood shop was his escape from his day job as a school bus driver. George could not wait to retire from that job. The older he got the less behaved the children became. The kids were rude, no respect for their elders, nor their peers. The kids were racist as well. A fact that was unnerving to George. He had dealt with his share of racism and thought that he and Paulette had overcome such barbaric ways. He was wrong. And the parents of the children, they were no help. Every child was a saint. Every child was misunderstood. It made George regret never having a child of his own, to be able to raise them right. However, that boat sailed off a long time ago.

George was born and raised in Valley Brook. It was a quaint little town in the middle of Long Island. All around the town commerce and development was booming. Valley Brook sat economically sound and free of all the hustle and bustle of modern life. This is one of the reasons why George decided against leaving the town. It was hard to leave the house that you built from the foundation up, and your wife, your lovely dear hearted wife, put her all into to making a home. How does one just leave that? George did promise himself that if the hustle and bustle of the world outside of Valley Brook spread into the little town that George loved so much, then yes, he would leave. But that was not the case. Valley Brook was not backwards, but it certainly was stuck in time. And that was comforting to old George.

George sat in his booth in the Valley Brook Diner. It was off in the corner of the diner. The booth was only a two seater, right next to the rest rooms. Most patrons and dinning parties would prefer to sit elsewhere. Sometimes they would even wait for the next available table, regardless if the two seater booth was open. For George, the tiny booth was just perfect. It had a window that faced out to the parking lot. Past the parking lot there were some trees where George would admire the animals, mainly squirrels and birds, engage in their playful routines. Past the trees were train tracks, where the LIRR would howl through Valley Brook. Ever since he was young, automobiles, planes, and trains always fascinated George. It came as no surprise that he would go on to have a career as a school bus driver.

George was a regular at the diner, as he made it a weekly tradition to have diner out every Sunday night. He just finished his meal, the regular that he always ordered, The Valley Brook Diner Turkey Deluxe. Better known as "the number 2". It was a fine sandwich with fresh thinly sliced turkey, lettuce, tomato, and a generous serving of bacon. The bread was George's favorite. It was made in the diner and was the best he ever had. The sandwich came with the diner's special sauce which George could have sworn was honey mustard, mayo, and a pinch of Sriracha sauce. It had just the right amount of spicy kick to it, as well as a savory sweetness. George was just guessing though. He was no chef, just a lover of food. The sandwich came with thick steak fries that were crispy on the outside and soft on the inside. And of course George ordered them with special sauce on the side. To drink, plain old ice water. Nothing fancy. Soda or sweet tea would get in the way of his taste buds relishing in the flavor fullness of the meal. Heaven forbid.

He never had coffee (he had one cup a day, at home) and he never ordered dessert. His excuse was no sweets, but the truth was dessert just reminded him too much of Paulette. It was her favorite part of any meal. It was a celebrated trait of hers. She would always order the richest treats. Cheesecake was her favorite. But she could never finish the dessert, no matter if it was cheesecake, a slice of key lime pie or gelato. Paulette would always beg George to help her finish it. And he would, without a hint of protest. After all, any food left behind was a sin.

"So how was your sandwich?" Linda the young waitress asked.

"Oh, you know," George said. "No one can come close to your homemade bread and that special sauce y'all use. Delicious as always, thank you." George said all of this with a gigantic smile on his face.

"Good!" Linda said, smiling back. "Good to hear, Mr. Mills. So, do you want any coffee?"

"Mr. Mills is my father, God rest his soul," George said. "And you should know better. Please, call me George."

Linda let out a shy giggle. She had the looks of a super model but the brains of a 9-year-old. George appreciated her respect though. He gave her points for that in his humble little book.

"Sorry, George! Sorry!" Linda smiled and shook her head. As she did, her brown hair caught the last rays of the sun just right. It glimmered and gave off the scent of strawberries. Linda rolled her brown eyes with a smile. "I'm in another world some days, I swear." George had to laugh. Linda was a good girl. She meant well and he knew that. Linda had a soft and sweet soul. It was rare to come by nowadays. Every visit to the diner she would also bring George the late edition of *The New York Times* for him to read. It was an added bonus for him. It was no wonder why Linda was his favorite waitress, hands down.

George returned Linda's pleasant smile. "No harm done, Linda my girl. And no, no coffee for me. Thank you. Going to go home, read and go to bed early. So, just the bill, please and thank you."

"Oh, sleep sounds great," Linda said. "I'm exhausted! Worked a double yesterday and looks like today will be the same."

"Well then," George said as he dug in his back pocket for his wallet. "Let me buy *you* that coffee. Sounds like you need it more than anyone."

Linda began to open her mouth to decline. George raised his hand in protest and continued. "Now I insist. It's been a while since I bought a pretty girl like yourself a cup of Joe. So just do me the honor and accept, please."

Linda smiled with watery eyes. She blushed a certain shade of pink making her look like a child's doll. It had been a rough day for her and she appreciated George's kindness. "OK. OK, George," she paused. "But, you do know that I get coffee here for free though, right?"

"Well, then go get yourself one of them fancy Starbucks then," George laughed with a smile.

Linda could not help but smile back. "That sounds delicious actually. Thank you. Really."

George took out some bills and placed on the table. "My pleasure, but please- this doesn't mean we are going steady, you understand? It is just a Starbuck."

Linda laughed. "No, no. Of course not. We are just friends. It is just a Starbuck."

"There you go," George said and chuckled.

"Well, can I get you some dessert or anything else?" Linda knew the answer, but she was just programed to ask this question after a guest had finished their meal.

"No," George said, waving his hand. "No sweets for me. Just the bill, if you would be so kind."

Linda giggled. "You got it, no problem." She handed him his check. In turn he handed her some bills. "I will be right back."

"Take your time," George said. Linda was off to retrieve George's change. On her way, she was stopped by a table of elderly women. There were four of them, four chickens clucking away about this and that and everything that did not matter at all. They talked bad about their husbands, and they talked even worse of the dead. They bragged about their children and grandchildren, each chicken trying to top the last chicken's story. They talked freely and in poor taste about immigrants as they bashed the "negro" president. George shook his head. Just about everything that came out of their mouths was negative, including what they had to say to dear poor Linda, that their food was subpar and her service was mediocre at best. To top it off, they wanted to speak to a manager immediately because the amount of black olives in their house salads was excessive. George sighed at their behavior and looked outside the diner's window.

The world was busy this evening. Cars drove to and fro. Everyone seemed to be in their own little special world. George smirked at the busy and unaware world outside. He marveled at how far everyone had come and yet how far they still had to go. He was amazed at how self-absorbed the world had become. How cruel it could be. The four chickens were proof of this. It seemed as if there was no longer any compassion in this world. Having dealt with racism his entire life, George was hoping for a change but the one thing that those chickens got right about "the negro president" was that he failed at uniting the nation. In George's humble little book, he failed with flying colors. It was a shame that those colors were red, white, and blue.

George had seen a lot in his time and he did not take any of it for granted. He supposed that was because he had lost so much in his life. He tried to stay positive, but it was tough. Out of everyone George had ever known and loved, he was the last man standing. For the last 3 years he had been nothing more than a recluse. He would only leave his house twice a week- once to do grocery shopping and the other, like today, he would visit his favorite diner. Two days out of his house was more than enough he felt. The rest of the week George would spend at home alone.

George was a recluse, not a shut in. The difference was plain- he could go outside if he chose to, however he just did not like socializing with humanity any more. It seemed to George as if humanity in all was taking giant steps backwards instead of forward. He wanted no part of it. Besides, there was peace at home. His neighbors were good people that kept to themselves and as the saying goes, good fences make good neighbors- he rarely saw them.

Other than reading, a majority of George's time was spent in his garden. He enjoyed weeding and planting and working on his green thumb. If the weather was bad, then it was just another excuse for him to read more. Mainly fiction, stories of space exploration and tales of horror and suspense. It was a nice escape from the modern world. Sometimes he would read sports non-fiction, always about Baseball, the only sport that he could ever care about.

Some days, though it was rare, George would even work on his house, if his old body let him that is. He had a bummed knee and his back was always giving him trouble. Nevertheless, George would still make "Honey Do" lists that he knew his late wife Paulette would approve of. It kept him busy. And to George keeping busy meant less time for socializing and such. George was 68 years old and had buried just about all of his friends and family. He no longer wished to get close to anyone in fear that they would leave this world, thus leaving him alone yet again. It just hurt too damn much.

Linda returned with his change. "Here you go, George. See you next week?"

George took the coin change and left the bills. It was a nice size tip. Linda could get a "Starbuck" for the next three days.

"Thank you," said George. "And yes. I will see you next week, my dear." He got up from the booth and did a little stretch. His knees cracked as did his back. He let out a moan.

"Linda, my dear?" he asked.

"Yes?"

"Don't ever get old," George said. "It's for the birds."

CHAPTER 2
YOU GOTTA BELIEVE....

It was Sunday night, dinner time at the old Valley Brook Diner and George was anxious for his meal. The diner was popping with customers and orders. Lucky for George he was able to get his same old booth and Linda as his server as well. He took his seat and settled in, admiring the busyness of the world around him.

"Hiya, George! How are you tonight?" Linda asked in a frazzled voice.

"Oh, I am good, Linda, I am good. How are you?"

"I am good, but wow, the dinner rush came early...!" Linda looked over at another table. It was a booth down the way filled with four blue haired wrinkled women. They were motioning for Linda. She gave them the universal symbol for one moment, a finger in the air, and drew her attention back to George. George smiled. He appreciated Linda and her hard work, as well as her patience with the pushy customers that she had.

"Here you go, George," she said as she put water on his table and slid the late edition of *The New York Times* towards him.

"Thank you, Linda," George said as he got ready to read his paper. "Well, you know what I am having. Same as always. The good old number two."

Linda frowned. "Sorry, George. Believe it or not we are out of turkey! We've been so busy today and the lunch rush totally wiped us out."

"Well. Ain't that something. Hmm. Well, what do you recommend then?"

"You might think I am crazy but the meatloaf is great here." Linda offered.

The thought of anyone but Paulette's meatloaf made George feel uneasy. "No, no meatloaf for me," George said. He ordered the first thing that he saw on his menu. "I'll take the number nine, please."

The number nine on the Valley Brook menu was the You Gotta Believe Burger. An all-beef patty with cheddar cheese, onion rings, applewood bacon and Valley Brook Special Sauce. Comes with your choice of one- French Fries, Cole Slaw, Potato Salad or Steamed Veggies.

Linda jotted George's order down on her pad. "Good choice! Do you want fries with that?"

"Linda, you should know the answer to that," George answered with a chuckle.

"Duh. Fries it is," Linda said. "Annnd a side of special sauce..."

"That's my girl," George smiled.

Linda giggled. "Basically, the same meal that you always get only this time it is a burger! Say, how do you want the burger cooked?"

"Oh, I think medium will do just fine."

"Sure thing. That is how I order my burgers, too," Linda beamed. "Anything to drink, George?"

"No, no, this water here is enough right now, thank you kindly."

"OK. I will be back to check on you in a bit. Thanks!"

"Thank you, Linda. But don't worry about me. I know you are busy. Dinner time rush and all."

"Yeah, it sure is," Linda was more than a little frazzled now. "Be back soon."

"Take your time, my dear," George said with a gentle smile.

George looked around the diner. He recognized some of the patrons but did not care to get up and make small talk with anyone. Shelia Klein, the old elementary school teacher, was eating with her husband David, the pharmacist and their granddaughter, Whitney. Shelia caught eyes with George and gave him a smile and a little wave. He waved back and immediately looked out the window.

George admired the trees; they were beautifully bare on this brisk October day. The seasons were on their way. It was going to be another tough winter of missing Paulette.

Before he knew it, George's meal came out. He was impressed by the food that was on his plate. The burger was a thick piece of meat. George was amazed by the thickness of the patty. The cheese was melted to perfection with a generous amount of bacon peeking out from the under the blanket of cheese. The bun was slightly toasted. George could see that the cook buttered the bun before he put it on the grill. A nice touch in George's humble little book. The appearance of the meal looked like something from the show Top Chef. The presentation almost made it too good to eat. George, however was famished, and the meal smelled delicious. He said a quick prayer of thanks for the food, placed the top bun on top of the burger and took a giant bite of the sandwich.

The taste was overwhelming. His tongue exploded with saliva as the juicy meat, the savory cheese, salty bacon, and the buttered bun sent his taste buds into a frenzy. George looked at the bite mark in the burger and examined the meal. Was this really just a plain old hamburger? It was delicious beyond any other burger he had ever had in all of his years. It was a pleasant surprise for George.

George picked up a fry. It was still hot to the touch so he gave it a little blow and then bit into it. The fry was perfect. Steak fries had always been his personal favorite and this portion of fries was exquisite. George dipped the giant fry into the special sauce. His taste buds once again danced with glee. The flavor of the salty fry and the gentle sting of the special sauce, as well as the texture of it all, was bliss.

George looked out the window mid bite and admired the car that just pulled into the parking lot. A 1969 Ford Mustang. It was a baby powder blue and was in mint condition. George let out a little whistle and took another bite of the burger. This bite had a pickle in it and the taste of dill really brought the meal together.

The driver of the car opened the door and got out. The man seemed to have been listening to a sporting event. George chuckled at the man's appearance. The driver of the car was wearing a vintage polyester leisure suit. It was a powder blue, as well, matching his car. The driver's hair was feathered out and fluttered in the wind. George smiled as he remembered that time, the time of hippies and of the civil rights movement. It was an exciting time. His smile faded as he looked down at his paper.

The paper was still *The New York Times*; however... the date read October 16th, 1969.

George shook his head at what he was seeing.

"You are losing your mind, old man," he whispered to himself. He then looked up to examine his surroundings, for surely this was all one grand joke that was being played on him. He rubbed his eyes in disbelief at what he saw.

The Valley Brook Diner was still busy, just as he remembered it was, but all of the patrons were dressed in late 60's and early 70's attire. The women wore their hair in that typical bee hive style. They wore pea coats and wool tights. Some had thick horned black glasses. The men either wore dress shirts and ties or button down collared shirts. Some men wore flannel shirts with slacks.

George looked back down at his newspaper. The headline read *VIETNAM MORATORIUM OBSERVED NATIONWIDE BY FOES OF THE WAR; RALLIES HERE CROWDED, ORDERLY.*

Under that, another article, *Protests Staged in Capital as Nixon and Aides Meet.*

"Nixon?" George whispered again to himself. "That son of a..." His voice faded off as he studied the paper more. He shook his head and squinted at the picture on the cover. Towards the bottom left of the paper was a picture of a baseball game.

"The world series..." whispered George. "Is that *today*? It's the game-"

George was interrupted by a shouting coming from outside the diner. He drew his attention to the commotion outside in the diner's parking lot.

"Hey, Jimmy!" a man yelled. "Is that the game?"

"You know it!" the man that drove the Mustang shouted back.

"Well, come on! Turn it up! One more and it is over!"

"I know! I am holding my breath that we take it all today!"

"Hey, man... you gotta believe."

"Oh, man, how groovy would it be to be at Shea now?"

"Far out, man!"

"Shh! Listen!"

The feathered hair man turned up the radio. Loud enough for George to hear and as he listened George was frozen in his seat. Was this a prank? If so, kudos to whomever had orchestrated it. It was flawless.

The radio voice spoke in a timeless voice- "Beautiful day here for a game and oh boy what a game it has been. We are entering the top of the 9th inning; the Mets are up 5-3. Koosman is on the mound, pitching a great game. Only 5 hits allowed today. Baltimore's line up is in the middle of it's batting order. Koosman will face Frank Robinson, Boog Powell and Brooks Robinson..."

I remember this! George thought. *I remember this game, this moment. I thought it was all over for poor Koosman. But that was back in... 1969. What a year 1969 was!*

The radio voice continued on- "Koosman gave up three runs in the 3rd and since then has shut out the Orioles. He has retired 16 of the last 17 batters, 7 of which were in a row." George looked around. It seemed as if no one was aware he was there. Everyone was going on about their business. George checked under his table and behind him, looking for a clue that this was all a joke. He found nothing to prove this. The voice on the radio continued.

"Robinson steps up to the plate. He has flied out to right, homered in the 3rd, struck out in the 6th and here comes Koosman's pitch. He takes the first pitch. Ball one, curve ball..."

It was as if George was 18 all over again. He found himself growing anxious as he listened to the ball game, even though he already knew the outcome of the game. Every New Yorker, sheesh, every *true* baseball fan knows how this game ended. It would go down in history as one of the most inspiring upsets in sports history.

The men in the parking lot moaned as Koosman walked Robinson. There was now a small crowd around the Mustang that was broadcasting the game. The crowded moaned along with the men, some vocalized their discontent.

"Take him out! Koosman is a bum!" a young man said. His hair was buzzed and he wore a white tee shirt and baby blue jeans.

"Shut up, Ray! You are just jealous cause your Yanks didn't get in!" another young man shouted over the sound of the radio. This boy's attire was identical to his friends, only he wore a New York Mets cap.

There was the sound of the crack of the bat. The crowd outside's attention went back to the voice on the radio as it described what was happening at Shea.

"Ground ball hit to second base, the throw is in time, Robinson tagged out." The crowd coming from the radio began to boo.

"Robinson tried to take Harelson out with his slide and the crowd here is not happy about that, but hey folks, that is how the game is played. Robinson is out, Powell on first. Brooks Robinson comes to the plate now."

"That must have been a dirty play!" a small boy, also with a Mets hat on, said. "They were really booing that fella!"

"Yeah," a fat man with a cigar began. He talked at the boy but never broke eye contact with the radio. "But like the man said, that is how the game is played."

"Wow, one man on and one man out. Koosman is in a real pickle!" the boy said.

"I don't think so, sonny," an old man in a suit replied. He was a negro just like George. George thought that he recognized him but could not place it. The old man continued. "Old Jerry is pitching a doozy. This game, win or lose, is going to be talked about for years to come."

The man on the radio announced a pinch runner for Powell whom was Chico Simone. George laughed at hearing the name for it brought back the memory of when George was into collecting baseball cards. Even though he was 18 back then and just a tad too old to be collecting, he did it anyways. He just loved baseball and collected cards to stay up to date with the stats of all the players. His mother hated the hobby. Once he left for the war, all his cards, all his Mantles, Robinsons, Mays, Clementes, Roses and Ryans went into the trash. Knowing their worth a few years later really hurt George but what was done was done.

George's concentration was broke now by the small crowd outside and the monster crowd on radio erupting in cheers. Brooks Robinson had flown out to right field. The Mets had one more out to make and then they would be the World Series Champs of the year 1969.

"They're going to do it! Just you watch and see!" the young boy said.

The feather haired man laughed. "Little dude, I hope so. Man! I would have done just about anything to see this game live at Shea!"

The rest of the crowed concurred. Even Ray, the Yankee fan, agreed that it would have been a treat to have seen this game unfold live.

George sat in his booth watching the crowd interact and talk to one another. It made him smile. All walks of life stood outside, gathered around a car, listening to a baseball game. All their differences were put aside. George giggled as the line "Root root root for the home team..." came across his mind. That was exactly what was going on outside the diner. It was almost as exciting to watch as the game itself.

The man on the radio informed his audience that Dave Johnson was up at bat now. That made George chuckle as he knew the fate of Dave Johnson. Dave Johnson in 1986 would be known as Davey Johnson, famous for managing the New York Mets to a dramatic 7 game World Series win over the Boston Red Sox. Another miracle year for those amazing Mets.

George felt like a little kid watching the crowd and listening on to the ball game. Part of him wanted to get up and place bets on what would happen next. He was destined to win some cash if he did but his good heart just would not allow him to exploit this precious moment to the small crowd. He decided it would be best to finish up his meal and once the game was over, at least go out and celebrate with the crowd.

The man on the radio described the next play, almost as if it was happening in slow motion. The pitch from Jerry Koosman came down towards the plate. Dave Johnson swung, and the crack of the bat could be heard as he connected with the pitch. The ball rocketed up and out of the infield. It traveled further into the outfield. The ball found itself in the mitt of left fielder Cleon Jones for the third and final out. The Mets had won, final score 5-3. They were the World Series Champions of 1969.

Even through the glass of the diner, the roar of the crowd on the radio was deafening to George. It gave him chills and it amazed him that he could even *hear* the crowd; he was near deaf and sitting behind a thick pane of glass as well. Nevertheless, the crowd on the radio screamed and cheered in sync with the crowd listening on the radio in the parking lot.

The fat man with the cigar hugged the inquisitive boy. The old man shook hands with Ray the Yankee fan. The two feathered haired friends exchanged high fives with the other man in the Mets hat. The entire diner exploded with thunderous applause knowing that their team had won.

And there sat George, grinning like a drunken fool as he took it all in. He thought to himself that if this was a prank, fine. He would get up and shake the hands of those that prepared it. It was well done. If he was dreaming, great. What a fantastic dream. A nice break from all the doom and gloom he was so used to. If this was all real, then he was thankful. To relive such a happy memory in such detail was a gift from the Lord above. And if he was losing his mind, then so be it. There were worse effects to losing your mind than reliving the final game of the 1969 World Series.

George looked down at his plate. About one more bite remained of the burger. He was excited to get out and celebrate some with the parking lot gang. He decided first to finish the delicious meal. It was too good to waste, and after all, any food left behind was a sin.

He chewed fast, in a rush to get outside and relive a special part of his own history (even though at the time of the Mets winning the '69 series, he was working as a janitor in the movie house. He listened to the game on a small radio in the closet. He still remembers the smell of the cleaning supplies. He also remembered even though the volume was as low as low could be, the crowd at Shea Stadium still bellowed through the tiny speakers). A waitress, not Linda, approached him and began to reach for his now empty plate.

"All done?" she asked with a little smile.

George looked up at her with a mouth full of food and nodded like a child.

"Well then," the waitress began. "Let me get this out of your way."

George offered her a smile and a nod. He hurried up his chewing. He looked down at the table as he reached into his pocket to get his wallet out. In his excitement, he lost grip of the wallet and it fell under the table. George reached down to retrieve his wallet and as he did the waitress took the empty plate off the table.

"Can I get you anything else, George?" a now familiar voice asked. George looked up with wide eyes. Did his eyes deceive him? Standing before him now was Linda. She held his empty plate up with a smile.

"Sheesh! Guess it is safe to say you liked the burger, huh?" She laughed. "You ate every last bit of it...!"

George looked around the diner in a panic. He looked outside for the celebrating crowd but there was no one. No one but a young couple getting into their car. A Silver Toyota Matrix. There was no baby blue 1969 Ford Mustang to be seen.

"You OK, George?" a concerned Linda asked. "You look like you have seen a ghost or something."

"Yeah, or something," George whispered. He cleared his throat.

"Just the bill please, Linda."

"Sure, George. Be right back."

Linda left George sitting in his booth looking confused and shocked. He looked once more out the window but it was the same as before. No Mustang. No cheering crowd. George slumped down in his seat. He looked around the diner and saw all the familiar sights that he was used to. Everything was the same as it was when first sat down. Everything was updated and modern.

George looked down at his copy of *The New York Times*. The date read October 16th, 2016.

CHAPTER 3
GRILLED CHEESE AND TOMATO SOUP

George could not sleep. What he had seen (had he really seen it at all?) kept him awake, full of curiosity and nostalgia. From the diner's window, he witnessed history. Or was it just a flash back? Did the food he ate trigger something in his brain to click and take him back to the year 1969? Was the beef tainted? Did the virus travel up to his brain and make him only think that the year was 1969? Could be, but with spoiled meat, especially beef, George knew that his stomach would have been in awful shape. This was not the case. His digestive system seemed to be right as rain. And over all, George felt great. The burger's taste was still on his tongue and he found himself craving more. Come to think of it, today's hamburger was hands down the best he ever had. So what gives?

George laid in bed all night. Tossing and turning. Thinking about the car. Thinking about its owner. Thinking about the behaviors of the people inside the diner. Their mannerisms and speech were of the old days. He was left alone to finish his meal. As he ate, it was 1969. Once the food was gone, everything went back to 2016.

George chalked it up to him getting older and his mind was slipping. That thought was scary, but it was comforting enough to help him finally fall asleep. Right before he did, he decided that he would have dinner again at the diner tomorrow night. And this time, he would have something other than his turkey club or the number nine hamburger.

* * * * * * * *

George came to find out that he could not wait for dinner and went to the Valley Brook Diner for a late lunch. It was a dark and drab day out. Just barely sixty degrees, overcast and wet.

George entered the diner and gave the hostess a hello nod and wave. As he made his way back to his booth he was relieved to see that Linda was working. *Good old Linda,* he thought. *She works so hard. It's admirable.*

George eased into his seat and looked over the menu. He looked over the specials and to him they did not seem all that special. Pasta and meatballs, fried chicken with brussels sprouts, the meatloaf. *Boy, they really push that meatloaf,* George thought. He looked outside. It was a gross day. The sky looked as if it was about to open up and down pour at any moment. The weather made it clear to George what he was going to have today for his early dinner. He scanned the menu and found what he was looking for. His stomach growled with anticipation of the meal.

"George!" Linda said as she walked over to his booth. "I thought that was you but just thought that my eyes were playing tricks on me! Two days in a row! Wow! What a nice treat!"

George smiled. He really did enjoy Linda's warm personality. "What can I say? I just cannot get enough of you, my dear," he played. "What a day it is out there, huh?"

"Oh, it is so yucky," Linda replied. "For once I am happy to be here!"

"I know what you mean."

"So, what can I get ya? The regular? Or you want to go for the burger again?"

"You know, I think today I would like to have the Grilled Cheese and Tomato Soup combo. Seems like a good day for it, don't you think?" George smiled.

"I do!" Linda agreed. "In fact- today for lunch I had a BLT with tomato soup!"

"Hey, great minds, my dear, great minds!" George said looking up at Linda. Linda smiled but looked confused. "Great minds," George began. "They think alike."

"Oh!" Linda blushed. "Yes. Thanks. Yes they do."

George caught on to the fact that he embarrassed Linda and changed the subject. "Linda, if you would, *The New York Times*, please," George requested. "Whenever you get the chance."

"Sure, I will get it right now... be right back."

Oh, I definitely embarrassed her! George thought. *George Mills, you goon. Better leave that girl a nice big tip. Again.*

George smiled and day dreamed about what this next meal would bring forth. He was giddy with anticipation. So much good history to relive. The moon landing. V-Day. Maybe he would get lucky and history would repeat itself again only this time, he would see the Mets win the World Series in 1986. Maybe he would see Paulette. This thought made him float. The chances were slim that he would see anything at all. He had no explanation as to why he saw what he saw yesterday. It could have been a fluke. Just a figment of his imagination. But nevertheless, even if the chances were low, to see Paulette again...

"Here you are, George," Linda said as she placed a glass of ice water and the late edition of *The New York Times* in front of him. "Anything else? Want some saltine crackers maybe? I like crackers with my tomato soup..."

George chuckled. Linda was a sweet girl. He really got a kick out of her. "Thank you, Linda, but I am alright for now. Thank you."

"My pleasure," Linda said. "Be back with your food as soon as it is up."

George nodded and looked at the paper. The date read October 17th, 2016.

As he waited for his meal, George flipped open the paper and saw the world in turmoil. He was taken aback by the amount of horrors that plagued the world. Terrorist attacks, robberies, murders, rapes, corrupt politicians. It was as if all of the world's comic book villains had come to life, but none of the super heroes. Where was Superman? Batman? Spiderman? Where was anyone with a kind heart anymore? George frowned and flipped the paper to the sports section. There was always comfort in the sports section.

The baseball season was coming to an end. The play offs were in full swing as the Cleveland Indians battled the Toronto Blue Jays and the Los Angeles Dodgers took on the Chicago Cubs. Although his Mets did not make it this far, George was still excited for the post season. He was hoping that the Indians would meet the Cubs in the

World Series, and then may the best team win. Both teams played a great season, although the Cubs, boy, were they due for a World Series win. It had been 100 years since their last World Series win. Regardless, George couldn't care less who won, just as long as it was a good series and not the Dodgers. They were a dirty team and George did not care for them. Ever since he was young, he never liked the Dodgers much. *Somethings never change* he thought.

"And here you go," Linda said as she held George's meal. "Grilled cheese and tomato soup. The perfect meal for a day like today." She placed the plate with the sandwich in front of him and the steaming red bowl of soup she placed towards the end of the table.

George closed the paper and put it towards the far side of the table. He looked at his meal. It looked divine.

"Thank you, Linda," George said looking at the food and then up at her. "It looks delicious."

"No problem," said Linda. "Chef makes a mean grilled cheese. I know it sounds funny, I mean, it is just toasted bread and cheese, but you just wait and see. It is top notch. The tomato soup, too, is awesome." She laughed. "You know, if I don't order the burger here I normally get this meal right here. Funny. We have the same taste it seems... great minds, right?"

"That is right, Linda," George said with a chuckle. "Great minds think alike."

"Enjoy!" she smiled.

"Thank you, Linda."

George looked down at the meal in front of him. Whoever "chef" was deserved a medal for his presentation of his meals. The grilled cheese sandwich awaited George upon a piece of parchment paper. All around it was garnish of leafy greens and a small ramekin of pickles. Whomever grilled this sandwich up knew what they were doing. The homemade bread was a perfect golden yellowish brown. The cheese oozed out like yellow lava. It was a thick sandwich. There was a generous amount of bread which on another sandwich would have been a waste; however, the extra bread in this case could be used to sop up the tomato soup. George lifted the sandwich with two hands and took a bite.

The texture of the sandwich was heavenly. There was a subtle crunch and then a tender softness that was followed by the sharpness of the cheese. The chef used butter on the bread as he grilled it, George was certain of this, for the taste was of fluffy richness. George took another little bite to witness the chewy cheesy savoriness once more. He then ripped the sandwich in half. The cheese stretched like a piece of yellow dough and finally snapped making the sandwich two parts now. George put one half down and the other he dunked into the tomato soup. The soup was thicker than George was used to and this sparked his curiosity. The sandwich soaked up the soup and George brought the sandwich to his mouth and took a bite.

George's eyes lit up as the combination of grilled cheese and tomato soup touched his tongue and awakened his taste buds. Hands down, the tomato soup was the best he had ever had. It was buttery smooth and had a flavorful thickness to it. It was sweet yet salty, almost like a gourmet marinara sauce, only not as acidic.

George looked out the window. It was a beautiful cloudless day. A welcomed change from the weather earlier in the day. He looked into the parking lot at the cars and it hit him that he was no longer in his time. It was no longer 2016, as the cars looked to be late 1950's. Big boat like vehicles with shiny chrome rims and head lights. To make certain he was indeed somewhere in time and that there was not just a local car show going on in the lot, he looked towards his newspaper. It confirmed his speculation- the newspaper read that the date was October 17th, 1959.

1959! George thought and smiled. He had done it again! Time travel! And to 1959! What a great time in his life. He was 10 going on 11 and his world was filled with wonder. His life was nothing but baseball and playing pretend. His best friend was Willy Monroe (God bless his soul, Willy would pass away in 1963 after getting hit by a train while playing on the tracks). George forced himself to look at the positive of this experience. It was 1959, it was a year that rang out in his head as being special. Special, innocent, but still, there was a darkness there. But why darkness? The reason escaped him as he took another bite of his sandwich. The cheese oozed in his mouth as if it were melting on his tongue.

George looked around the diner. Did this place ever change? It looked the same as it had always, except for the patrons of course. George chuckled at the fashion sense of the 50's as he remembered them well. The women with their dresses, mainly floral prints, looking like wearable wallpaper. Some wore their hair in tight perms, others wore their hair pin straight, primped up at the bottom. The men looked sharp in their dress shirts and ties, covered by cardigan sweaters. Their slacks were tailored to their body and their shoes were all shined to look like new. George remembered his shoes back during that time; they were sleek looking as well. He recalled with a smile that his parents always stayed on top of him to keep his shoes clean. He dipped the sandwich back into the soup and then took a bite. He marveled at how much simpler life was back then. As George chewed he looked outside, and there she was. The most beautiful woman George had ever seen.

Up until today, this moment right now, George had only seen her face in photographs. Even in the photos she was heavenly. A true woman, a sultry goddess that was taken too soon- Dorothy Pine. George, like everyone else in his community, knew all about Dorothy Pine. They did not know her as a person though- what they knew of her was the *tragedy* of Dorothy Pine. Dorothy was at the wrong place, at the wrong time, hell, in the wrong *decade* as far as most were concerned. George included.

George could not take his eyes off of her. George smiled and felt butterflies in his belly. He felt 13 all over again. It was like he was seeing a celebrity. A ghost. A goddess. Dorothy was a legend.

What George felt looking at her took nothing away for his love for his dear Paulette. He would much rather see Paulette, no contest, but seeing Dorothy live, in person, walking and breathing, it was a sight to see. Like seeing a tyrannosaurus rex or a sabertooth tiger, alive and well in front of you. It was mesmerizing. The way Dorothy walked demanded attention, and that is exactly what she got. However, not all attention is always good.

As Dorothy walked towards the diner, George saw three other faces that he recognized, and the butterflies in the pit of his belly caught fire and turned to ash. The world suddenly moved in slow motion. Like watching a car accident, or your buddies get gunned down in the jungles of Vietnam, it is a dream like feeling. What was about to unfold, however, George knew was nothing less than a nightmare.

The faces that George saw were those of Butch Duggan, Billy Conrad, and Bobby Brock. Too many they were innocent boys "defending themselves". To others, like George and his community, they were nothing but murderers.

George watched with eyes wide open. Dorothy walked towards the diner. The three thugs took notice of her. They nudged each other. They chuckled. George could smell their testosterone.

It all happened in slow motion and George held his breath the entire time.

As Dorothy passed the low lives, Butch's hand flew out from his side and grabbed a handful of Dorothy's rear end. Without missing a beat, Dorothy's hand flew from her side and found Butch's face with a loud slap. Dorothy was stronger than she looked, as Butch's head snapped to the side. A drop of blood peaked out from Butch's lip. Dorothy continued her way towards the diner.

"Haw!" Billy said. "You gonna let a nigger do you like that?" Billy and Bobby both chuckled at Butch's expense. Butch turned red. He reached out and grabbed Dorothy by her shoulders, turning her around towards him. He was a hulk holding a rag doll.

"Who do you think you are, huh?" Butch spoke through his teeth.

"Get off of me!" Dorothy cried out. "Who do you think *you* are?"

"No one hits me like that, spook," Butch said. His pink tongue came out and lapped up the blood. "Especially no broad. Especially no nigger broad."

"Get off me!" Dorothy demanded.

"No," Butch whispered. "No, I don't think I will." He continued on to grope Dorothy putting his hands all over her body. His hands found her breasts and he squeezed. Dorothy cried out in pain. Butch pressed himself against her and began to put his hands up her skirt, grabbing and squeezing Dorothy's behind. Billy and Bobby joined in as well.

Billy grabbed her backside, in competition with Butch's hands. Bobby squeezed her face, making her lips, her beautiful lips, pucker up. He played with her hair, running his fingers through it and smelling it.

"Damn," Bobby said. "They got weird hair, don't they?"

Butch scoffed. "If you say so. I am more interested in *other* parts." He then pushed Dorothy back and in the same motion he ripped her blouse open. Her bra and soft belly were exposed. To

Butch's surprise, Dorothy's leg flew up and into his crotch. Butch cried out in pain as he held his privates. His face was red with anger and pain. His eyes teared up. Dorothy wasted no time and clawed at Butch's face, leaving deep scratches on his face that would end up leaving scars. This act was the justification of the boy's so called innocence... Dorothy had assaulted Butch.

Butch had enough and made it known by swinging a mighty fist into Dorothy's gorgeous face, dazing her and breaking her nose at the same time. George marveled at the sight. Even Dorothy's blood was beautiful.

Dorothy fell to her knees. An embarrassed Butch in a fit of rage and pure hatred began to kick her. And as if on cue, Billy and Bobby joined in.

Dorothy collapsed to all fours.

And they kicked.

And they stomped.

And they *grinned* with sadistic glee.

Dorothy's petite body was no match for their hateful kicks. George could stand no more. He stood up at his booth and slammed his fists on the diner window. The patrons inside watched appalled. At *George*.

"Stop it!" George cried out. "You're killing her! You're killing her!" The patrons all looked at him, then and out the window, and then back at George.

A woman with curly blue hair shook her head. "Tsk tsk," she began. "This is exactly why they have their own section." She did not even bother to whisper this statement. In fact, she said it as a matter of fact and with pride.

The man she sat with had a scowl on his face. "Yup," he said looking back at his plate of meatloaf, mashed potatoes, and green beans. "They are nothing more than animals." The man stabbed his fork into the meat loaf, crammed it in his mouth and chewed. He then continued. "Nigger girl is just getting what she deserves."

George looked at the couple horrified. He had not heard that term in years. *Nigger.* A funny word, used by those that think they have class and culture, yet when they use that word, they sound like uneducated goons. And to think that Dorothy was getting what she deserved... it was ludicrous. No human would ever deserve to be given such a beating. No creature on earth for that matter.

Outside, the three men were now kicking and stomping the beautiful Dorothy. George could see that she had had enough. She was all but limp. Every once in a while, her hand would reach up and out towards them, a sign for them to stop. They ignored her and soon the men were kicking what seemed like a lifeless body. Or were they? George saw that Dorothy had just enough strength to try and crawl away. She dragged her broken legs behind her, leaving a trail of blood like a slug at midnight.

Still, they kicked.

Still, they stomped.

Still, the patrons in the Valley Brook Diner did nothing.

This would not pass for George Mills. For the first time since the war, he felt a cold rush of hatred and adrenaline. His heart raced and he knew what he had to do.

George made his way out of his booth in a hurry. Too much of a hurry, as he knocked his grilled cheese sandwich and tomato soup off the table. They crashed to the floor making an awful racket and mess. He was not as young and nimble as he once was, as he found his feet slide out from under him, thanks to the spilled tomato soup. George went crashing down to the floor along with what was left of his meal.

George laid on his back, feeling the sting of defeat. There was no way he could get out there and save Dorothy. It was too late. But he had to try. He had to at least dish out some justice to those three racist sons of bitches. Those three goddamn murderers.

"George! Oh, my! Oh, my!" Linda exclaimed. "Are you OK?"

Overcome with emotion, George pushed Linda to the side.

"I am fine!" he shouted. "Goddamn it, I am fine! I got to get outside... Where is..." He did not finish the sentence, for he already knew the answer. *Where is Dorothy?* Dorothy was dead. She had been for nearly 60 years. And her murderers? Brock, Billy, and Bobby? They beat the case and went on to live long lives filled with opportunity and family.

And the cold cruel realization crept into George's mind- he was back in 2016. He looked down at the floor. What was left of his meal laid there, scattered amongst the glass of the plate and bowl in which they were served. In his clumsiness, he knocked the plates off the table. The meal was then over. And so was the trip back in time.

"George?" Linda inquired as he sat on the diner floor. She knelt down beside him.

George pressed his lips together. "I am sorry," George said to Linda. He put his hand on her shoulder and gave it a little squeeze. "Sorry for hollering at you. Guess... guess I am just embarrassed about, you know, being such a clumsy oaf."

"It is fine, George," Linda said with concerned eyes. "Really. You need not worry about it. You are OK though? That was a pretty bad slip there."

George smiled at Linda. "Yeah," he said simply. "It was quite the fall. But, thank the good Lord, I am OK." This was a lie. There was a searing sting in his knee. He had twisted it pretty bad in his rush to get outside and save Dorothy. George thought it over and felt foolish. What was he going to do if he *did* get outside? Take on 3 young brutes and save Dorothy Pine? After all, he was just licked by a grilled cheese sandwich and a bowl of tomato soup for crying out loud.

"Well, good," Linda said, though she sounded unconvinced. "I am glad you are OK, but why don't you take a seat? You know, just relax for a moment."

George was already rattled by what he saw back in 1959, and now with all the patrons' eyes on him, he just wanted to go.

"No, I am fine, Linda," George lied. The pain in his knee throbbed, but the pain in his heart and his soul, burned like an inferno of woe. "Thank you. Just the bill please."

"You want some dessert to go? My treat," Linda offered with a smile.

George forced a laugh. He helped himself up and spoke through his teeth. "Thank you. That is mighty kind of you, but no. No sweets for me. Just the bill, please."

"Sure," Linda said as she dug around in her apron. She took out her little notebook and ripped George's bill from it. She handed it to George who barely looked at it and gave her a fifty-dollar bill.

"I will be back with your change," Linda said as she started over to the cash register.

"No, no, thank you," George said as he waved his hand. "Keep it."

"George!" Linda gasped. "This is a fifty!"

"I know, I know," George said. He smiled at Linda. "My body ain't what it used to be, but my eyes are aces. I want you to have that. Thank you again."

"George! This is too much!" Linda cried.

"Nonsense," George said waving her off. "I want you to have it. Really. It is my... it is the least I can do."

"George, you really don't have to do this," Linda said.

"I know, I know," George responded. "I just want to."

"Thank you, George, thank you!" Linda beamed.

"Don't mention it," George said. "I will see you, Linda. And thank you again, too."

George did not wait for a response as he left the diner just as fast as he could. His knee roared with pain and now his back was beginning to chime in as well. George felt like he had been hit by a train. He made it to his car, got in with a terrible groan, started it up, and pulled out of the Valley Brook Diner parking lot.

George cried the entire way home.

CHAPTER 4
HUNGER STRIKE

George could not find sleep at all that night. Whereas the hamburger meal kept him awake with excitement and wonder, the grilled cheese meal, or more so what he witnessed, kept him up all night with fear and horror.

To help him sleep, George decided to put on the TV. This, in retrospect, was an awful idea.

What was on? Nothing. The same old nothing that had been on for the last 60 plus years of George's life.

Channel 2, News- reports of a school shooting in a small town in Tennessee. 3 dead. Children. The next story was breaking news on a pedophilia sex trafficking ring that was busted up down in Florida. The ringleader of it all was an illegal immigrant. Reports of children from ages of 3 months to 10 years old. Over 30 children in total. Kept in cages like livestock. That was when George changed the channel.

Click

Channel 3, static. Peaceful until George really looked at the picture. Tiny little dots. Black and white dots, danced upon the screen. The longer George watched, the more it looked like the dots were fighting. More black on white violence, more white on black violence. George changed the channel.

Click

Channel 4, a late night show. Laughter. A thin man in a suit, the host, making fun of the president. Same jokes that have all been said before. The host's guest was a young girl that had gone viral on the internet, whatever that meant. Small little thing. No older than 13 with the mouth of an adult. A disgrace to women, a poor example of a human being. Her mouth was vile. She did not make sense to George.

Click

Channel 5, a cartoon. More filth. Making light of pedophilia. Mocking religion. Ripping apart family values and traditions. Disgusting entertainment.

Click

Channel 6, infomercial. An overly excited female trying to sell some contraption that cleaned bathrooms with little to no effort. Too good to be true.

Click

Channel 7, the news. Same shit, different channel. Racism. Murder. Rape. Molestation. George turned off the television and sat in the darkness.

Is this it? George began to think. *Is this the best we can do? Racism? Murder? Rape? Pedophilia? What has changed*, really *changed in the last 60 plus years? Nothing. It was always a struggle. Always resistance. Always oppression. Always hate. Always murder and rape and theft and....*

George was tired. Not physically. Not even mentally, but soulfully. He was drained. Who was he kidding? What did he have left to live for? His wife, Paulette, was dead. He was the only one of his siblings still alive. He rarely ever talked to his nieces or nephews. His friends all died off one by one. Cancer, heart attack, stroke, diabetes. And if they weren't dead or dying they were living in some assisted living home which was just an appetizer before death. *What was the point of all of it all?* he wondered. *You live, you love, you work, you die.*

George had had enough. He did not accept the funny little life rituals any more. No, to George, life was more than all of that. Somewhere along the line, he had missed it. All of humanity had missed it.

George watched the sunrise, a sight that normally brought him great joy. It was the sign of a new day. A new start. A chance at getting it right. But today's sunrise hit him with a sour touch. Everyday is a new beginning, indeed, and yet it is wasted by so many. Wasted on hate. On ignorance. On lies and greed. All George wanted to do was to feel Paulette's kiss. He wanted to hear her laugh. He wanted to see Dorothy Pine smile, see her fall in love with a boy, get married and live a life full of love and goodness. George did not want to hear about war. He did not want to picture another child being hurt. He did not want to hear news of a rape or any other fiendish sex act. George wanted peace. But George was old enough to know now that these were all just pipe dreams. These things would never come to be. No matter what he ate and saw at the Valley Brook Diner- humanity was doomed.

As the sun continued to climb up into the sky, George sat emotionless in his *Lay-Z-Boy* chair. He stared outside his window at the passing cars and mothers pushing their children in strollers. He got up and went to his desk drawer in the next room. There was his army issued 1911 Colt. He picked the gun up out of the desk drawer. It was heavier than he remembered. He racked the slide. The gun was now loaded. He placed the gun down upon the desk top, amongst bills and books. He looked down at the pistol.

"Hiya, Georgie boy," the gun whispered. George remembered that whispered voice from back in 'nam. George did not answer. The gun continued to speak.

"All alone again, huh?" the pistol teased. "Brings back memories, don't it?"

George frowned.

"Ah, you remember!" the gun said. "Bac To. The battle, ahem, the slaughter of Bac To. Remember, Georgie boy? Your entire platoon was killed that night. It was just you and me and what, 10? 12? How many Vietcong bastards did we drop together? Come on now..."

"Nineteen," George whispered.

"Nineteen! That is right!" the pistol cheered. "Nineteen gooks we killed that day! Remember? Remember? Remember that word, Georgie? Gook? Funny word, huh? Sounds funny... and it *is* funny because here you are, thinking about the world and woe is me, poor me, boo-fucking-hoo and what? Did you forget? Did you forget that *you* are a murderer? 19 is a whole lot of bodies to stack, Georgie boy."

"That was... different," George answered.

"Different!" the gun laughed. "Different he says! How is it different? Murder is murder, pal. Murder is murder."

"No. It was survival," George spoke softly.

"Survival!" the gun howled. "Survival the man says!"

"Leave me be," George moaned.

"Murder is murder, Georgie boy," the gun jabbed. "Murder is murder. Say. You remember that one we shot together? Remember it? You know the one."

"Shut up," George whispered, his eyes teary.

"You do! You do remember! You remember pulling my trigger, my muzzle lighting up the night. We saw what happened. Bullet caught that young VC right in the kisser!" the gun laughed hysterically. "Remember his face just *exploding*? Oh! And remember what you were doing? Remember you were holding, ahh, what was that white boy's name... McMillan? McBregger? McMick?"

"McMalley," George answered.

"McMalley!" the gun cried out. "McMalley! That fucking mick! Remember how he would pray all the time? Remember that? If it fucking rained out, he would pray. He would pray for his meals, pray for his family back home in, what, Chicago?"

"Yes," George confirmed somberly. "McMalley was from Chicago."

"He was young, too, wasn't he? 18? 19?"

"Barely 18."

"Damn, that is young. Too young to die in such a way," the gun continued. "Remember how he died? He was the last one of your platoon to bite it. VC got him with 10 rounds right into his face! Remember how all you could see was just one of his eyes, staring up at you... the rest of his face was red jello with teeth, but he had that one eye... that one goddamn eye....and it looked up at you for compassion. For remorse. Remember? You held him and he died in your arms and do you remember what you said when he finally gave up the ghost?"

"I don't know, I don't remember," George's voice was uneasy. He began to sweat. "It was too damn long ago."

"My ass," the gun scoffed. "You remember. You remember."

"I don't..."

"Well, *I* do," the gun said. "You said 'Good. One less fucking cracker now...'" the gun giggled. "Oh, good times, Georgie!"

George hung his head. "I think we are done here."

"Oh, are we? Are we?" the gun laughed. It was a hideous laugh. It made George cringe. His insides felt sour. The gun continued.

"*You* said that. Not me. I know no color or race or creed. I only know bang bang, kill kill, death death. *You* said that to McMalley and then what? We went on that amazing killing spree! 19 dead! You went through so much ammo... you never were the greatest shot. Murder is murder, Georgie. And to top it off, you are a racist, too!" The gun giggled.

George was silent, and in his silence, he spoke in volumes. The gun sighed. "Well, shucks. I guess we *are* done here after all. Hey. It was certainly nice catching up with you, Georgie Boy."

George picked up the gun and placed it into the desk drawer. He stared down at the weapon. It was old. It looked tired. Just like George. He was old. He was tired. His knee was on fire. His back ached. His heart trudged on. He needed sleep.

Next to the gun George noticed the letter Paulette wrote him on her death bed. There it was, out in the open for all to see. It was short and sweet, just like his Paulette.

Dearest Love George,

Thank you for being by my side during this horrible time. I could never express to you how much I love you. Without you I am lost, and anything that is lost is only destined to die. With you, I feel alive. I feel safe. I love you with all my heart and cannot thank you enough for the wonderful life that you have given me.

Love with all my heart, always,
Paulette

"Aww," the gun broke the tender moment and memory. "She was something special, that Paulette. You got lucky, Georgie boy. She was *way* outta your league."

"Do you ever shut up?" asked George.

The gun laughed. "Go to bed, George old boy. You look like shit. Don't worry though... we'll meet again, Georgie Boy," the gun said. "Let's just say you ain't gonna see 2017!" The gun laughed a wicked laugh and George slammed the drawer shut.

George made his way upstairs to his bed. It was almost 9 AM. He had been up all night long. He had no problem sleeping, but before he fell asleep George realized that the gun was right... Paulette always *was* out of his league. He *was* a racist and a murderer (murder was murder). George also knew that he would never see the year 2017. Nor did he want to.

CHAPTER 5
A BETTER TOMORROW BEGINS TODAY

December 3rd, 2016. It had been a month since George had gone to the Valley Brook Diner. Tomorrow would be Paulette's 63rd birthday. George sat in his recliner chair looking closer to death than alive. To say that George looked like pounded shit would have been a compliment. He had gone close to two weeks without so much as leaving his home; the same could be said for showering and shaving. He did not even bother to celebrate Thanksgiving this year. What was the point? What was left for him to be thankful for anyways? His health? What a joke. Ever since the grilled cheese meal his knee had been severely swollen and his back pain kept him up all night. He lived off of whatever was in his cupboards which next to nothing. Saltines, cup of noodles, fruit cocktail and a few cans of beans and black olives. To drink, tap water. And even though it did not agree with his stomach, alcohol. Lots of alcohol. That helped him get some sleep, but even when he found sleep there was no peace, only nightmares. That day and night he saw Dorothy Pine haunted him and now the world was crashing down in all around him. He was sick and tired. Lonely, sick and tired to be exact. He thought of suicide more and more. His gun talked to him regularly; however, George had come to be in a catch 22. He had found out that he was too strong to off himself, yet he was too weak to go on any further. Besides, what was there to live for? Paulette was gone. In his eyes, the world was a steaming pile of shit. If he ate a bullet for dinner tonight, who would miss him?

Something poked at him though. Something he had not felt in quite some time. Was it hope? Perhaps it was common sense? Whatever it was, he decided to shower, shave, put on a nice suit and go to the Valley Brook Diner, for what would be his last meal. One last turkey deluxe perhaps? What would happen then? Would life just continue on as it was meant to? What if he had the burger again? Would he have happy memories again? Or would he just be having a burger in the year 2016? Nothing more, nothing less? What if he had the grilled cheese again, and this time, as soon as he saw those three punks he and his gun took care of them? Then perhaps Dorothy could go on and live a life worth living. What if he had missed his window though and he was still in 2016?

2016. Oh, how he wished it was any year *but* 2016. A year of despair. Sure, the years behind him had their bumps and woe, but they still offered some hope at least. Even after the war. Even after all of the deaths. Even after the death of Paulette, he remembered it hurt, oh did it hurt, but there was still a little hope. And a little was sure as shit a lot better than none, which was all 2016 had to offer. He would take 1968, the year he met Paulette. 1976-The year he married her. 1999, the year of the silly Y2K panic. He even would take 1971, face down in the rice patties getting shot at by the Vietcong, those mother fucking commie bastards. He would take 2001, watch the twin towers fall all over again. He would gladly take 1951, the year of his birth. Maybe he would write himself a letter... cliff notes as to where he will fuck up. Then maybe, he could get things right. Hope. This is what hope was. And that is what was lacking in George's life. Hope. And love. Maybe it was not too late. Maybe George could still find it. Maybe he could find hope and love still.

Love. The word tore through him like a Vietcong solider emptying an entire AK-47 magazine into his gut. Love. All the word did was make him think about Paulette. His soul mate. She was his life and now she was were gone. What was left for him? In a loveless world, how could he ever be loved? How could he ever expect to feel love again? A retired bus driver. A black male. Alone and unwanted. The cards were stacked against him. But still, the word love and this strange sweet sensation filled his heart. Was it Paulette? Was she working her magic from beyond the grave? George smirked.

Tonight- in honor of his late wife, he would have dessert at the Valley Brook Diner...

And then he would come home and blow his brains right out of his skull.

George showered, shaved and put on his navy blue suit that Paulette loved on him. George then stepped outside and made his way to his car. The weather was a typical winter day on Long Island. Gray sky yet no clouds and yet no sun. It was as if the sky was a drab blanket of sheet metal. It was a brisk 35 degrees out. George breathed the winter air in. It stung his lungs. His belly rumbled.

"Don't worry, old friend," George answered. "You're in for a treat. And then when we are done, I will have mine."

* * * * * * *

George entered the Valley Brook Diner and was greeted by Debra the hostess.

"Hi, sweetheart!" the peppy hostess eyed George up and down. With a smile she said "Boy! You are looking sharp today!"

George was in a sour mood. He felt bad, but all that he could offer Debra was a simple nod. He made his way to his booth. As always, it was open. He sat down with a frown on his face.

Just as he got comfortable in his seat, Linda made her way over.

"Hey there, stranger! Good to see you!"

George looked up at Linda. Sweet, sweet Linda. He could not be sour towards her. She had always been so kind to him. He smiled at her and folded his hands.

"Hello, Linda," he said in a gentle tone. "How've you been?"

"Good, good. Just busy. How are you doing? It is so nice to see you! You want your regular tonight?"

"Good to hear and thank you. I am doing fine. Just fine," George lied and then continued. "No. No, turkey deluxe for me. Tonight, tonight is going to be different. Tonight, I want dessert."

Linda laughed. "Dessert? George, you've been coming here for years and after every meal I offer you dessert and tonight, you start-off with it? Are you feeling OK?"

George chuckled. Sweet, sweet Linda. She was a good kid. He was going to miss her.

"I am feeling fine, Linda my dear. Just fine."

"Well, that is good. You look great by the way... what is with the suit anyways?"

"I've got... an important meeting tonight," George said with a smile.

"Really? Tonight?"

"Yup," George replied. "Tonight."

"Is it a date?" Linda said, half playing.

"Oh, heavens no. Nothing like that. Just a... meeting. About my future."

"Well that still sounds exciting," Linda said. "So, what will it be? I can recommend-"

George put his hand up to stop her and spoke. "Thank you but no need. I know what I want. I would like a chocolate milk shake."

"Chocolate milk shake!" Linda said with a smile. "That is my favorite!" Linda jotted down the order. "One chocolate milk shake, coming right up."

"One more thing," George said.

"Yes?"

George pointed over at the dessert display. "Slice of that New York cheese cake. The one with the cherries on top."

"Wow!" Linda said. "Milk shake *and* cheesecake! I am impressed, George!"

George chuckled. "Did you know that was my wife's favorite dessert? Cheesecake. Every Valentines and anniversary I would get her a pie. It never got old for her. It was a fun tradition."

"I did not know that," Linda said with a soft smile. "She loved Cheesecake *and* she married you? I'd say she had great taste."

"She did OK," George said. A flash of his wife in her wedding dress flashed in his mind. She looked beautiful that day. She was always looked beautiful. Paulette's beauty was timeless. George missed her.

"I will be back with your... meal," Linda said smiling.

"Thank you, Linda."

"Oh! I nearly forgot!" Linda said looking up at the ceiling as if asking for help. "Your paper. Here you go."

"Thank you again, Linda," George said. Linda gave him a tiny smile and went off to put George's order in.

George touched the newspaper but did not bother to open it. He only looked at the date. December 3rd, 2016. The date made his insides quiver. George had been on this earth for 65 years. And what? What did he have to show for it? No grand legacy. No bloodline. No attachments. He fought in a war, a bullshit war. He worked a job, a bullshit job. He collected a pension, a bullshit pension. It was all bullshit. It was time for George to move on. It was time to put this world, this life, this bullshit behind him. It was time now for the last course. It was time for dessert.

"Here you go, George," Linda said as she put down the milkshake. It looked delicious. The glass was tall and frosted. The liquid inside was the perfect shade of chocolate brown. A generous amount of whipped cream and two cherries on top. Linda placed the slice of cheese cake down next. "And the cheesecake." She slid the plate in front of George. "Enjoy, George! I will be back in a few to see how you are doing."

"Thank you, Linda." All that George could smell was the sweetness of the desserts. The delicacy of it all. The slice of cheesecake jiggled on the plate, enticing George to take a bite.

George offered Linda a kind smile as she made her way to help her other tables. George eyed the dessert in front of him. The smell of the cake's decadence, the overwhelming sweetness of it, made George's mouth water. The cherries were plump and smothered in a thick red fruit sauce. Paulette would have been ecstatic to dig in to this culinary masterpiece. George decided he would start with the cheese cake first, in her memory. Just a taste. Just a taste would do. The rest, the rest would be for her. For his love, Paulette.

George's fork cut through the cake. The cake made a soft sound of separation. George brought the fork up to his mouth. The smell was enchanting. He put the piece of cake in his mouth. The cheesecake was one of the best he had ever tasted. The creamy texture of the cake made his taste buds explode. Whoever baked this cheese cake knew *exactly* what they were doing. It was top notch. They dusted the perfect amount of graham crackers on it. And although looking at the dessert one would think the baker went overboard with the cherries and the fruit sauce, it was indeed the perfect amount. The cheese cake went down his throat, smooth and satisfying. George felt a slight touch of regret that he passed up so many opportunities to have the dessert. In retrospect, he really missed out.

George put the fork down as he looked around the diner. Nothing different. It was all the same. He let out a gentle sigh and took in all of the hustle and bustle. It was all bullshit. He was born and raised in this little town. He had seen so much in his time. He had watched people grow. He had seen people be born. He had seen people move away, disappear into the wakes of life. He had seen people die. Too many. George had seen enough. Enough of it all. Enough of the bullshit. He needed a change.

George pushed the plate of cheese cake away. He pulled the milk shake closer to him. He looked straight down at the dessert drink. He dared not look outside. He did not want to see what this meal brought. He just wanted to enjoy the moment. George moved the milk shake towards him and took a sip. It was beyond delicious. It was absolute heaven.

The taste brought back memories of a better time for George. A time where there was hope in his life. Hope and love. How Paulette would always finish her slice of cheese cake and then steal a sip or two of his milk shake. She would do it with that sweet little smile of hers. Oh that smile of hers... George would do anything to see it, just one more time. Just one more time.

He took another sip of the milk shake. The second sip was even more satisfying than the first. It coated his throat and gave him a chill throughout his body. George smiled as he decided to let his curiosity get the best of him. He looked out the window. The sip of milk shake he had in his mouth never made it down to his belly. George stared outside with his mouth a gap, chocolate shake dripping out and down upon his suit.

Outside, the sun was out. The sky was clear. Clear, except for the flying cars. Flying cars and what looked like flying *people*. George began to clean up the milk shake mess that he made as he leaned towards the window and studied a man, flying with what looked like a jet pack of some sort. There were no flames coming from the pack, but the air around him was distorted. The man flew through the sky with the ease of a bird. The more George looked, the more flying people he saw. They wore jump suits and helmets. There was no disarray; they flew like a flock of birds, in complete trust and harmony of each other.

Outside his window, a flying car landed right in front of George. It had no wheels, yet it moved upon the ground as if it was hovering.

The flying car came to rest on what looked like rubber bumpers, reminiscent of those of a helicopter. The car was sleek, shiny, and chrome. Not a scratch or ding on it. No dirt, dead bugs or anything. It was pristine. George could not see who (or what) was driving the car for the windshield was pitch black. Then, like the wings of a swan, the doors opened to the vehicle. First, the driver stepped out. A healthy looking young man. He was dark skinned. Not black, but not quite anything else. He was a good-looking man, too. Handsome as an actor. He jumped out of the shiny machine and ran to the passenger side. There, he offered his hand to the passenger. Out came one of the most beautiful girls George had ever seen.

The girl had pin straight thick black hair. She was light skinned. Not white, but not quite anything else. She had eyes that matched the color of the sky. Her outfit hugged her body. It was form fitting, accenting her curves in a tasteful way. She seemed to glow in the sun. Radiate. The man took her hand and with a smile helped her out of the vehicle. Both the man and woman looked at each other with love and respect. The man waved his hand at the car and the doors fell shut.

"This is the place I was telling you about," the man said as the couple made their way to the diner's front doors. "My grandfather used to take me here. He used to take my dad here too. I have a lot of great and special memories of this place. I wanted to share it with you before we leave."

The woman hugged the man and kissed him gently on his coco butter colored skin. "Oh, Langston... it is adorable."

"It really has not changed," Langston said. "They even have the same menus!"

"Thank you for taking me here," the girl said. "You talked so highly of this diner; it is nice to finally visit it."

"Wait until you try the food," Langston said. "It is not the same as the food on Venus, but it sure comes close!"

"You know me, I just love food!"

"Come on then," Langston said guiding the girl by her hand.

"Let this be our last meal on earth!"

"Oh, I am just so excited!" the girl squealed. "Tomorrow we leave for Venus!" She smiled at her man, Langston. It was a sincere smile, one of undying love and hope. "I love you, Langston."

The couple shared a kiss. It was a kiss of innocence.

"I love you, Victory Grace," the man said back. "Come on. Let's eat."

George smiled at the sight of the two lovers. Two good looking kids about to take the journey of their lifetime... a trip to Venus. George thought about that... Venus! He scrambled to find the paper to see the date. He read it once. He read it twice. He shook his head and read it four more times. Then he whispered the date out loud.

"December 3rd, 2092...," he looked again outside the window. The world before him was gorgeous. The sky was clear. The clouds were as white as fresh snow. The buildings were amazing. They looked the same as what George was used to, but they were built with solar panels and wind turbines upon them. In fact, as George looked around, there were no more telephone poles. No more electric wires that dangled black strings across the neighborhood. The streets were no longer paved; they were instead, huge solar panels themselves. And they were spotless. No litter. And the landscaping of this time was surreal. The grass was a deep lush green. The trees still had their green leaves which was alarming to George as it was December still; the paper in front of him had said so. *The paper!* George thought.

He moved his milk shake over and began to inspect the newspaper. It was still *The New York Times*, but the paper... it felt different. It felt thinner. And it smelled wonderful. George chuckled as he read the headline and shook his head.

NYC MAYOR TO SIGN OFF ON TAX ELIMINATION BILL

There was a picture of the mayor, a woman, whom the caption said was named Tomeka Parks. "Mayor Parks," George whispered. "Good for you, ma'am. Good for you."

Like a child on Christmas morning, George flipped through the paper and was beside himself with joy. The world, some way or another, had made a total 180. Where there once was hate, there was now love. Where there once was war, there was now peace. Where there once was famine, there was now abundance. There seemed to be no more oppression. No more chaos. No more innocent lives lost. The world had woken up. Humanity was now one race, the human race. Science had made diseases obsolete. Now, humanity set its gaze upwards towards the stars.

The sports section, however, was where the real astonishment came about. According to the paper, The Long Island Mets had signed the top relief pitcher, Jessica Thompson. George beamed with amazement. He read the article on this acquisition by the 'mazing Mets, it seemed that Jessica was practically untouchable. Last year she played for the Red Sox and her ERA was 0.92 with 149 strike outs. The Mets had signed her for 102.9 million dollars, for 3 years. Last month, she turned 24 years old.

George read more in the sports section. What a time it was in the sporting world! Females were more active in the professional aspect of it all. They were rather common in the MLB as well as the NFL and NHL (George read about a goalie named Cassandra Tsvolski that played for the Cleveland Rockers. She was the shoe in for MVP this hockey season. She lead the league in shut outs, earning her the nickname "The Great Wall of Cleveland".)

George sat back in his seat. He felt out of place, yet, he felt at home. The Valley Brook Diner had minor changes here and there. New light fixtures, new hostess stand, new front doors. George scanned the patrons of the diner. They were all dressed *nice*. The women wore clothes that complimented them. Nothing revealing, nothing obnoxiously tight. Plain and simple yet classy all the same. The men dressed with the same classiness as the women. Their clothes were well tailored and pressed. All of the men looked like they were important. Like politicians or lawyers, but *tasteful*. Once again, the word classy came into George's mind.

The couple from outside came into the diner. They were seated a few booths in front of George. He was able to get a better look at them. They were a good-looking couple. They looked well rested and ready to take on the world, Earth or Venus. They sat across from one another, excited to be in each other's company. Excited for their future together, a future filled with hope and love.

George sat in his booth smiling. His eyes had tears in them and he wiped them away. He took a sip of his milk shake and then moved it back towards the window. He blew a kiss to the plate of cheese cake.

"I love you, Paulette," he whispered.

George was approached by a waitress. She was a gorgeous girl. She looked to be of Indian decent. Again, not quite black, not quite white, but stunning nevertheless. Her name tag read "Lorena."

"Sir, is everything OK with your meal?" Lorena asked. George took a moment to admire her beauty. Her big brown eyes, her silky black hair, smooth olive skin. She smelled fresh, like a new born.

George gave her a smile. "Oh," he began. "Oh, yes, everything is fine. Just fine, thank you. I just need to step outside... just for a moment. I will... be right back." George smiled and got up from his good old booth.

"OK, sir," Lorena said. "Take your time."

"Oh, I think I will, thank you," he said without looking at Lorena.

"We will keep your seat," Lorena smiled and began to take Langston and Victory's order.

George walked towards the diner's doors, towards the world outside. The sun shined into the diner, its rays a gentle yellow and white. George acknowledged the hostess with a gentle nod. He put his hands on the doors to the diner. He stared outside the doors, at the beautiful day that was a mere few feet away.

George opened the doors to the diner.

He closed his eyes and breathed in the fresh mild winter air. With a smile on his face, George walked out of the diner and into the new world.

-THE END-

ABOUT THE AUTHOR

Justin Joseph is an author. An artist. A father.
A husband. A son. A brother.
A friend. An enemy. A saint. A sinner.
Some call him Invi,
while others never call at all.

www.JustinJosephWrites.com

Other works by Justin Joseph include

-The Halloween Kids
-They Come from the Mountain
-The Deadly Woe
-Ghosts! Zombies! Monsters! Bunnies! 13 Tales of
Woe and Wonder (part I)
-Ghosts! Zombies! Monsters! Bunnies! 13 Tales of
Woe and Wonder (part II, with Amanda Torroni)

Children's Books (written under the name Mr. Invi)

-Our Friend Mr. Bacon Nose
-Mr. Bacon Nose Goes!
-Monster Defense 101
-The Incredibly Amazing Super
Fantastic Narwhal Man!
-Little Baby Bigfoot
-Good Night, Starboy

+ + +MORE COMING SOON+ + +

Made in the USA
Columbia, SC
23 February 2019